Gushers

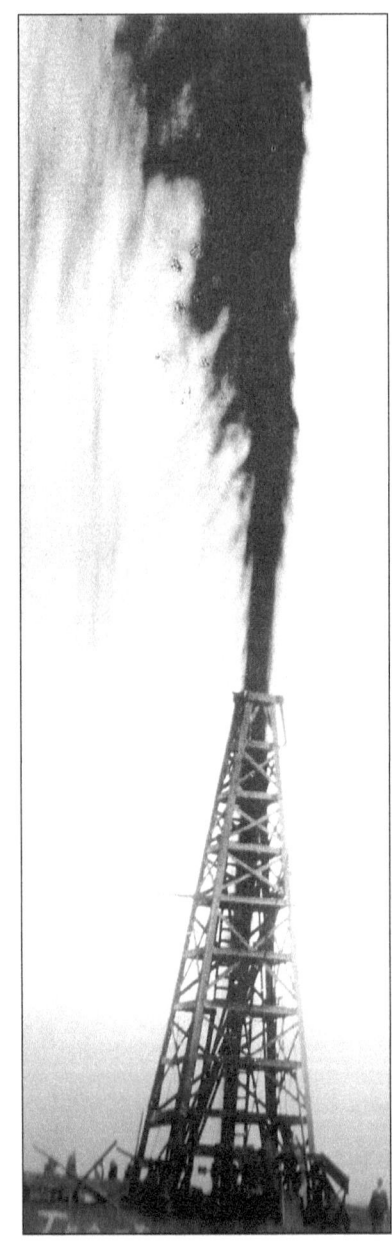

Gushers

Oilfield
Novels of Texas

Dick Heaberlin

A Cavalcade of Oilfield Novels

Orange House Books
San Marcos, Texas

For additional information
visit the author's website at
DickHeaberlinWrites.com.

Copyright 2009 by Dick Heaberlin

ISBN 978-0-9794964-5-5

For Joan

A Cavalcade
of Oilfield Novels

This is the second of my survey of novels written about work and life in America's oilfields. *Fountain Wells* chronicled the novels about the early oilfields in the East and in Canada. *Gushers* surveys the many novels written about Texas oilfields.

In the last year we have seen the price of a barrel of oil go from over one hundred and forty dollars to just forty. In *Fountain Wells*, I review novels that told the stories of people caught up in, enjoying, and suffering from these wild fluctuations. The stories are similar in the novels about Texas oilfields.

When I took a course in the English novel in college, I discovered a wonderful resource: Edward Wagenknecht's *Cavalcade of the English Novel*. From reading it, I was able to put the novels I read in context of other works written at the same time, many of which were rare and unavailable. I hope with these books to provide a similar service. Many of the oilfield novels I survey in these volumes are rare. I can provide this survey only because I have been persistent in finding these books on internet sites such as Abe Books, Alibris, and Amazon. I also have had available to me the remarkable collection of the Perry Castaneda library at the University of Texas in Austin.

In *A Cavalcade*, I describe and discuss the important novels written about oilfields from the first one in 1876 to those of the present. I've arranged the material chronologically within the area of the oil-fields, beginning with the earliest ones in the East. Most of the early novels are set along the wooded creeks and hills of Western Pennsylvania, a land of small farmers and lumbermen. I've followed the movement of the oilfields west to Texas. Then I will move to Oklahoma, and from there to the Western States. It's quite a tour.

I want to make readers aware of a relatively un-known segment of our literary history. I rarely pro-vide literary criticism, for readers may have little in-terest in it until they know of these works and have an opportunity to read them. I focus more on the scenes in the oilfield and less on the financial deal-ings and the lifestyle of those wealthy from oil.

Contents

Oil Novels
of
Coastal
Texas

Chapter 1

Never-Never Land

From the mountains of Western Pennsylvania, many of the seasoned oil men made their way to the Southeast Texas coast in January of 1901 when the Lucas Gusher blew in at Spindletop, just outside of Beaumont. The quantities of oil coming from the Spindletop wells was much greater than that from the Eastern fields and led to the end of Standard Oil's monopoly. After Spindletop, there were many other strikes along the gulf coast, some of the first were in Sour Lake, Batson, and Humble. The events occurring in these fields have found their way into several oil novels. The best of these novels are different from other oil novels because they deal realistically with the particular complications of drilling in an area of high rainfall and rank vegetation.

The first oil novel supposedly set in Coastal Texas, Gertrude Potter Daniels' *Eshek The Oppressor* (1902) is an unbelievable melodrama. Daniels had set her first oil novel, *The Warners* (1901) in the East. In it she attacks the oil trust, particularly, John D. Rockefeller. In *Eshek The Oppressor* she continues her attack on the oil trust. We assume that the Eshek of the title represents someone in the villainous trust, but ironically there is no Eshek in the novel. Indeed, there is no single person to fight against, only the practices of the group.

We have a central figure that we follow from his youth to middle age. The novel begins with Jarvis Kennedy's having been laid off from his job in a factory in the north. He has found no work, is out of money, is cold, is alone, is despondent. Desperate, he steals a purse with $35 in order to buy a train ticket to California. Another thief tries to take the purse from him, and in the struggle that follows he knocks the man unconscious. On the train he reads a paper and discovers that the man he hit has died. But before he died, he wrote a letter to his brother, Gilson Meredith. Jarvis assumes he would have put in the letter information that would allow someone to track him. To throw pursuers off, he leaves the train early. As he travels, he meets a family with a female child. The husband first and then the wife die. Before she dies, she asks Jarvis to take the responsibility for raising her daughter, Theo. He accepts the responsibility along with her remaining money. This is all done in great detail with great emotion and lots of exclamation points.

Three years later Jarvis takes the money Theo's parents had and buys oil land in Flaremont, Texas. He is lucky in that his land is the pick of the county even though he is not an expert. Interestingly, Daniels reports, "As if true to his convictions, the West had given him his opportunity. It came abruptly, unexpectedly, but big with possibilities. The discovery of oil in Texas was one of those startling, unlooked for occurrences that have marked each era of this Western country's progress." (*EO* 80)

The problem is that the only two oil strikes in

Texas before this book was written had been in Corsicana, in East Central Texas, and in Beaumont, on the Neches river near the Louisiana border, neither of which are in the West. Since the name is Flaremont, one might assume Beaumont is the intended place. The Lucas Gusher in Beaumont in January 1901 was the greatest single discovery in the history of oil. The gushers at Flaremont are described by Daniels: "One had but to sink a shaft to become a producer. Then suddenly the earth around Flaremont could not wait for drills and shafts. Time and again great geysers of oil broke through the surface, thrusting themselves into notice, spouting high in the air." *(EO 80)* This and the events she describes fit the scene in Beaumont rather well: "Companies were organized of all grades of good and evil, for the benefit of those outside the state. Hundreds of men flocked to the town, endeavoring to get a foothold in the new industry without the expenditure of capital. Stock was sold broadcast. Circulars explaining the condition of affairs and inviting inspection were widely distributed." *(EO 81)*

The narrator next describes a typical boom town but finishes it with cowboys and Indians: "Cowboys raced by attracting attention to themselves, riding to create an impression, shooting their revolvers in the air and laughing at the women's screams. Indian women, highly painted, stood stolidly watching the throngs, chewing tobacco, smoking, exchanging stories." *(EO 82)* There were no cowboys and Indians at Spindletop. Instead, there were Afro-Americans, Cajuns from Louisiana, Scots Irish hunters and moonshiners from the Big Thicket, and farmers from the red dirt hills of East Texas.

The narrator describes a scene that never was: "In every direction oil derricks were in evidence, rising like somber guardians of the prairie lands. Invariably, little homes lay resting under their very shadows. New adobe structures, muddy white, with vine-covered porches, very shady and cool under the wilting glare of endless sunshine, were set about like so many dots on the landscape." (EO 83) Beaumont is on the coastal plains, but so near the piney woods that it wouldn't be called prairie land. There are lots of vines there, but no adobe. Those adobe structures would not fare well under the sixty inches of rainfall that Jefferson county gets each year. Derricks were closely packed with pine shanties below in the mud and oil. What Beaumont had in abundance was mud and mosquitoes and humid heat and fever — malaria and oil fever.

Another thing that never was is the fight that the independent oilmen have with a large Eastern conglomerate. Standard oil's Texas subsidiary, Waters-Pierce, had been thrown out of Texas in 1900 for violating Texas anti-trust laws. Standard had some refining capacity in Texas but were by no means dominant, and one of the directors of Standard has been frequently quoted as saying, "We're out. After the way Mr. Rockefeller has been treated by the state of Texas, he'll never put another dime in Texas." In fact, Standard's share of the national production of oil remained high, but it was lessened in large part because of the great flood of oil coming from Southeast Texas. New companies were formed there. Refineries were built in Beaumont and Port Arthur. Pipelines were built to Port Arthur, and oil was sent out from there by ship. Control of rail prices and cars would not keep the flood of new oil from reaching the market. And *Eshek The Oppressor* is primarily about the need for the independent operators to join together to fight the trust.

There's a lot more melodrama here as the plot comes to a weird end. The oilmen decide that the answer to their problem is a political one. They put up John Jarvis as Senator. Surprisingly his opponent is Gilson Meredith, the Eastern machine's man. Meredith, the brother of the man Jarvis accidentally killed, has moved from California. When he hears the name Jarvis, he somehow and miraculously remembers the name in the letter and concludes that Jarvis is the man who killed his brother. How the deceased man would have known Jarvis' name is not explained, nor how his brother could conclude that the two Jarvises are the same. Anyway, he does. And Jarvis, feeling guilt, quits the campaign. A warrant is put out for his arrest. He explains to his friend Calister that he doesn't trust the courts: "Yes, but you forget we are up against the trust. The trust that controls those very courts and laws and judges and juries. Meredith is simply the mouthpiece of the X. & Y. The road is but the cat's-paw of the Eastern Petroleum Company." The novel ends with an absurd pseudo-scientific resurrection that has nothing to do with the oil business.

Chapter 2

Muck, Fever, and Fire

In *Fever in the Earth* (1958), William A. Owens provides a vivid description of oil drilling in marsh and mud, showing us life in the Spindletop field as well as the nearby Sour Lake and Batson fields. Owens[1], already a well-known folklorist and collector of folksongs, interviewed many of the veterans of Spindletop during and after the celebration of the 50th anniversary of the Lucas Gusher. He and Mody Boatright included material from these interviews in their *Tales From the Derrick Floor* (1970). Historians of Spindletop have been greatly in his debt and have used his interview materials extensively in their accounts.

Owens built his protagonist, Hale Carrington, on the model of many of the men he interviewed, and Hale is the archetypical hero of an oilfield novel. He is an innocent, hard-working farmer who comes to the oilfield, learns quickly, endures hardship, illness, and dangers, grows proficient as a driller, and becomes a rich, successful producer. Then he tries to live with his success.

One month after the Lucas Gusher, in February of 1901, Hale Carrington leaves his poverty-strick-

[1] Owens (1905-1990) a folklorist and novelist and long-time professor and dean at Columbia University is best known for his autobiographical work, particularly his extraordinary *This Stubborn Soil.*

en farm in San Augustine in northeast Texas and heads south to the oilfield, hoping for a job and a better life. Just outside of Beaumont, he meets and teams up with John Ivens, an itinerant preacher, who is usually called Preacher. They arrive in Beaumont, already a boomtown, and meet an old man, who prophesies doom: "Gentlemen, I'm here to tell you they didn't have the right to turn such a force loose on mankind. It'll be a ruination. You mark my words. It's all right for man to do what he can on top of the ground, but when he gets down under, he's where he ain't got no business monkeying. You watch what I tell you. Beaumont'll live to regret the day drill was ever put to earth here." (FE 21) The old man shows them some yellowed houses: "They was white as snow the day the geyser came in. Now look at them. Look at the yellow. Rotten sulphur yellow. Nearer the well, they're beer-bottle brown. If they's enough evil in Beaumont oil to do that, they's enough to wipe us all off the face of the earth."(FE 21) Preacher seems moved by the prophecies, and Owens puts the title of his book into the last of the old man's pronouncements: "They's a mark on the land—a fever in the earth. The evil is on the people," the old man shouted. "Look at them. They come and go over the face of the earth—here today, gone tomorrow. Boomers. They ain't a-caring. You watch the people off the train. You walk out Crockett. You'll see what I mean"(FE 22)

Hale and Preacher find a place to sleep. Then Hale sees and is impressed with a young girl who is singing in one of the nicer saloons. She is Gaither

Ware, also a newcomer to Beaumont. She has just come there from DeRidder, Louisiana, where she had taught school until the school had closed because of a shortage of funds. Out of work, she has accepted a singing job working for her deceased mother's only brother, Jim Hanrahan. Hanrahan is one of the villains of this novel. He runs a high-class operation but is willing to do almost anything to anyone in order to turn a profit. Shy, clean-living, but vital, Gaither is startled to discover that she is to sing to a loud crowd of oil workers and oil promoters. Hanrahan dresses her demurely and keeps her away from his patrons. She resides in a house on Calder Avenue, where the aristocrats of Beaumont society live, and she is picked up and taken there by her own driver each day. Hanrahan gives her the stage name, Loretta Lee. Hale sees her and falls in love with her and remains so despite her odd behavior toward him.

Hale and Preacher get a job on a ditch-digging crew. The crew is racing against time to put in a pipeline to carry off the huge amounts of oil already thrown up by the gushers. Hale is now called Bo, short for Boll Weevil, the name given to newcomers from the farm. Bo and his crew work extremely hard:

> In all the changeable weather of the Gulf Coast — in days of chill dampness, in days of bright sun — they dug on, turning shovelful after shovelful of black gumbo and red clay, working sometimes in marshland with mud above their ankles, at times for short stretches on mounds

that raised them above the muck. Wagons and pipe stringers followed after them, and then pipe fitters and pipe layers, sinking the pipe into the raw wet earth.

Some could not keep the pace — or would not. A man would slam his pick or shovel against the earth with an oath and demand his pay. Bo barely took time to watch them leave, solitary figures walking across the prairie toward the boarding-house. Some refused to get out of their cots in the morning, and were gone at dinnertime. (FE 66)

Bo and Preacher dig the ditch and are hired to guard the sixty-five acre lake of oil to prevent the people crowding around from starting a fire. As they walk toward the new job, Preacher and Bo discuss their views of oilfield life. Preacher says, "It's a quare kind of living." And he says, "It's got a get up and go about it I ain't seen nowheres else." Bo says, "They keep a feller hustling."(FE 69) Neither is willing to give it up.

They are given guns and told to shoot if necessary to protect the lake of oil. Preacher says he couldn't shoot anyone, but he might throw the old pistol at someone. Soon the lake catches fire: "The opposing fires, moving steadily closer, made a giant whirlwind. The air began to swirl around and around. Smoke and flame rose higher and higher. The whirlwind, cyclone in force, lifted hot oil from the lake and, spinning it, shot it high into the air, where it caught fire, burst, and trailed down in echoing explosions."(FE 74) Preacher then says, "It's like the Last Judgment."(FE 74)

The fire finally burns the lake dry, and Bo and Preacher have a chance to talk about what they have seen:

> "That's the beatingest thing I ever saw," Bo said as they walked.
> "Nothing could be worse, outside of hell itself."
> "Do you recollect the old man we saw when we first come?"
> "He talked of trouble?"
> "Yes. I've been thinking about what he said. Not that I agree with him. It was man that let loose that lake of oil. In a way, it was man that started the fire. But it's man that's to blame. Not the oil. Not the fire. As I see it, man's just got to watch himself in the presence — not lose control —"
> "If he does, he'll suffer the vengeance." (FE 74)

On the walk to town, they reach a rig where the crew is sorely in need of temporary help. They pitch in, and Bo learns a lot about how a rotary rig operates. He finds out that driller is the best job, but that you have to begin as a roughneck.

They get ten dollars in pay and head for Beaumont. Bo again hears Loretta Lee sing and even requests the song she sang the first night, "J'ai passé devant ta porte."

Bo gives up his job on the pipeline and goes looking for a roughnecking job. Preacher stays with the pipeline. Most operators want to hire roughnecks with experience in Pennsylvania, Ohio, or Corsicana. One man asks Bo if he has had experience, and he remembers how hard he has been working digging ditches and remembers the words of a roughneck: "It ain't hurting nobody to fudge a little." (FE 89) So he lies and gets the job, at twice the salary he has been making. As a boll weevil, he has to endure the practical jokes of men in his gang, but he picks up the mechanical part quickly. He seems to be a natural at this work. He compares this job to his earlier one:

> Hour after hour they worked, quietly, humorlessly most of the time, constantly adjusting themselves to the needs of the machine. Bo missed the talk of the pipeline work, the singing and whistling. He learned to shout to make himself heard above the clank of pipe, the rattle of chain links on gear teeth.
>
> The work was different, and he began to understand the difference. Dirt work had been like farm work. He had been able to set a pace with his own body. But on the rig, it was the rhythm of the rotary, turning, grinding, steam-driven, all-demanding. A man counted as long as he could give in to it. (FE 90-1)

A nearby well gushes, and Bo moves in to rescue a man who has fallen from a derrick after being overcome by fumes. They put out their boiler to keep it from igniting the gushing oil. The other crew is working to install a gate valve, but they have to pull back from it at intervals because they are overcome by the oil. Soon people from Beaumont arrive:

Within an hour sightseers clogged the road from Beaumont and crowded around the well, watching the grim-faced men on the derrick floor, laughing and talking as if they were on an outing. Women ruined their skirts and shoes in oily mud, mud-soaked grass. Men risked death by gas for a closer look. They clapped each other on the back and spent their money frenziedly. The field was proved.

The driller, his throat raw from gas and yelling, set up a onestrand barbed-wire fence around the well and stationed armed guards around it.

"Make them stay back. If they won't, shoot to hurt," he ordered.

They stayed back, but their curiosity was not satisfied. In droves they tramped over the prairie. To see better, they crowded derrick floors of rigs close by. Men in business suits began scrambling up derricks. (FE 96)

One of those coming out is Loretta Lee. Bo, soaked in oil, tries to talk with her, but she ignores him. Then he decides that she probably hasn't recognized him, all covered in oil.

When Bo's crew tries to restart drilling, they discover that their hole has become clogged with quicksand. They have to skid the rig and start over. When the new well comes in, Bo is on the double board in the derrick: "The stream caught him in the face with drowning force, with sickening smell. He dropped his gloves and with bare, oil-lathered hands lowered himself down the timbers, foot by foot, forced to move slowly, afraid to be slow — a match, a spark from the boiler, would send the derrick up in flames." (FE 103)

They secure the well after it blows itself clean. But the well owner, Mr. Terry, opens it up again so that he can impress possible investors. The wind comes up suddenly, and the oil almost catches fire. Stang, Bo's boss, tells the crew to shut it down. Bo says that he was never so scared in his life, and Stang agrees. Bo didn't think Terry had the right. He begins to think of Preacher and of the old man: "The old man was partly right. Oil could be a ruination, if a man let it get out of control. The danger had not been so much with the oil as with Terry." (*FE* 106) But Terry's trick works, and he sells all the stock he wishes. Bo gets a bonus. He says, "It ain't no gift, if anybody had struck a match —" (*FE* 107)

Bo takes his money and buys himself nice clothes, "tapered trousers, loose-fitting jacket, white shirt with black string tie, and high-topped black shoes. He completes the outfit with a wide-brimmed panama hat, one like his grandfather wore. Wearing his new clothes, he manages a brief conversation with Loretta Lee, just as she is embarking in her carriage. She too has a new hat, and he says, "I gatlins, we both got new hats." (*FE* 110) He is pleased with even this brief conversation, pleased that he is neither bashful nor backward. Before he returns to the oilfield, he mails a letter to Loretta.

Shoemate, Bo's driller on Stang's gang, is bringing his wife to the oilfield from Pennsylvania, so he rents a house and invites Bo to rent a room with them. The room is not much to offer: "There were no windows. Light from cracks between the boxing planks made stripes across two cots. In the highest

part of the room Bo's head almost touched the raf-
ters. The roof sloped down to a side wall shoulder
high." (FE 117) Bo says that it is better than the derrick
floor and agrees to share it with Jonesy, another
member of their crew. There is a good description
here of life in a coastal oil town:

> Around them there were dozens of houses,
> no better, no worse, all hastily thrown together
> to accommodate men who had risked bring-
> ing their families to the oilfield. There were also
> tents, some with dirt floors, all leaky and damp
> and dirty gray from the rains blowing in from the
> Gulf. Sallow-faced women and hook-wormy chil-
> dren lived and worked and played in the smell of
> crude oil and open privies.
> "It's unhealthy country," Shoemate said.
> "Mighty hard on men and mules. It's harder on
> women and children. Too low. Too damp. You
> seen how your washing sometimes don't get dry
> and gets mildewed. Some of these folks must feel
> mildewed to the soul." (FE 117)

Then we learn about the dangers of living in
Gladys City: "They lived in gnawing fear of explosion, fire, death. Some showed their worry in their
faces. Some lived with a placidness made possible
by a fundamental belief in predestination: what is
to be will be, and no man may help it." (FE 117) Shoemate is worried about how his wife will adjust, never having lived anywhere but in the hills of Western
Pennsylvania

Bo wants a driller's job, and Stang will not give

him one, so Bo quits and starts walking from rig to rig looking. He finds a job, but he has to delay moving in with Shoemate because the job requires him to move to a marshy area south of the main field. Conditions here are described in detail:

> It was far off the road to Port Arthur, in marshland that turned to a bog in summer rains. They could bring in supplies only on days when the sun baked the marshes dry. When it was wet they were marooned, unless they wanted to go out on foot. It was desolate and still except for the occasional cry of a water bird or the night howl of a coyote.
>
> They laid a board floor on the mud and stretched a tent above it. By day a blazing sun made the tent a steamy oven. At night they set rag smudges to smoke out the mosquitoes. Only for a brief period in the afternoon, when a cool breeze blew in from the Gulf, could they feel refreshed. *(FE 129)*

The crew almost immediately begins coming down with malaria. They take massive amounts of quinine but continue to sicken. Bo does a good job managing his small crew, but nerves are raw and tempers flare. Shoemate tells him about how bad the disease is over the whole area: "You ain't been here to see how many's been taken down with malaria. They say the Hotel Dieu is so crowded that every inch of floor space is filled with cots. They can't get enough doctors. They're dying like flies. Funerals just about make a steady procession to Magnolia Cemetery." *(FE 131)*

In spite of all the hard work and sickness, the well is a duster, and again Bo is out of work. He catches on as a roughneck, but soon he is sick himself. While working ill upon a derrick, he observes a phenomenon — multiple gushers simultaneously: "He watched Spindletop go wild with excitement. Safety precautions were forgotten. Four streams of oil sprayed derricks and ground and spread into lakes. Sightseers waded through the oil and tropical rain. Crews on other rigs went right on drilling, their boiler fires an invitation to death." (FE 136) In the midst of this he has chills and the shakes from his malaria, and then the drill pipe begin to rattle. His driller hollers and tells him to get down: "In a kind of slow motion Bo begins the long descent down the derrick timbers. He knows the well may blow any second and take him with it. But he doesn't dare go faster. His body trembles. His fingers barely hold his weight. His friends grab him and help him down the final few feet. Immediately, the well erupts, making five wells gushing simultaneously.

Bo becomes so ill that Shoemate has to take him home to San Augustine to recuperate. As they are leaving, they are attacked by huge swarms of mosquitoes, blown in from the marshes. Bo says that he will never return, but Shoemate assures him that he will — that it's in his blood now. Shoemate insists that once he gets to feeling well he will be back.

And he does return several months later, healthy and determined to succeed. He has read everything in the newspapers about the oil business, particularly about how Beaumont oil has changed so much.

He sees Loretta again, but she brushes him off. Bo catches on as night driller on Shoemate's well. After it comes in, Bo and Shoemate start adjoining wells simultaneously. And soon they discover that they are racing. Terry offers a $500 bonus to the driller who finishes first. People take bets on the outcome. Bo's crew wins. About the same time the well blows in, a norther blows in, and the temperature drops immediately. Terry invites the winning crew to a steak dinner at the Crosby Hotel and provides tickets to *The Prisoner of Zenda* at the Opera House. After the steaks, Bo goes to visit with Loretta while his crew, Blackie and Jonesy, get drunk. At Loretta's he is warmly received and invited back for Christmas Eve, the next night. But when he returns to his crew, he discovers that Blackie has disappeared, and Bo receives a message that he must hurry back to the well because the extremely low temperature is causing the pipes to freeze. He and Shoemate work throughout the night and are able to prevent any damage to the wells.

Bo is awakened the next day by the sheriff. The sheriff has found a body floating in the river and believes that it is the body of someone seen at the Crosby with Bo. Bo is able to identify the body as Blackie's. Blackie had his bonus money on him the night before, and someone had killed him and robbed him, not an uncommon happening according to the sheriff. No one knows Blackie's full name or whether or not he has any family. Preacher is sick and cannot say any words over him, so after Blackie is placed in the grave, Bo says simply, "He was a damned good roughneck." (FE 166) Because Bo has to bury his man, he misses the Christmas Eve party on Calder Avenue.

Hanrahan had previously discouraged his niece from seeing Bo. But now he hears about Bo's new fame in the oilfield as a fast driller and encourages Loretta to see him. Hanrahan has created a company, DeRidder Oil, to dupe unsuspecting investors. He has no good oil leases, but he has a good front. He thinks Bo may be used as part of that front.

Bo is determined not to be just another working stiff for the rest of his life, so he persuades Shoemate to go in with him to buy a rig so that they can become independent contractors. They learn about someone who will have to let a rig go back to the Sabine Supply company if the well being drilled is a duster. Bo goes to the well and talks to the Old Pennsylvanian who is drilling it. Bo feels sorry for him because he is so old and overworked. The well is a duster, and Bo and Shoemate are able to buy the rig for $3,000. They are worried, but they immediately get a contract to drill a well, and their business is off to a good start.

On New Year's, Loretta tries to get Bo to go to work for Hanrahan, but he tells her he has just begun a business for himself. Bo's driver, Clem, warns him about Hanrahan, but Bo is already inclined to be suspicious of him.

When the anniversary of Spindletop arrives, many of the workers leave their jobs to go to the saloons to celebrate. Bo even decides to shut down, but he stays at the well and works during this unusual quiet time:

> When Shoemate had gone, Bo fired the forge to sharpen a fishtail bit. As he worked the bellows, smoke from the blacksmith coal clouded the derrick floor and shut out the smell of oil with a clean smell that reminded him of freight trains in the piney woods. He could almost hear a lonesome whistle blowing through the night. He held the bit in the fire until it was a bright red. Then he threw it on the anvil and with a twelve-pound sledge shaped out a new bevel. In the quiet of the oilfield, the hammer rang and reverberated with a sound that made him glad to be at work. When the bit was reshaped, he dropped it, hissing, into the tub of water. He tested the warm metal with his fingers and glanced along the bevel. Ne'er a man at Spindletop could do it better, he thought.
> (*FE* 193)

Shoemate and Bo bring in the well, get more contracts, and are offered loans to buy more rigs. They decide to be cautious and buy only one more, and Bo decides to leave Shoemate doing the field work and to search for opportunities to make some big money. He takes a small room in the Crosby hotel and starts learning about the oil business from the other side. Bo dresses up and hangs out at the exchange. He briefly tries his luck as a speculator, trader, and gambler, but he decides none of these is for him. He asks about Loretta from her driver, but he doesn't see her. Owens uses an oilfield simile to show Bo's uncertainty about her: "She is like sheen on a slush pit all aglow. You try to take a-hold and she's all changed." (FE 206)

Bo studies maps of the area and decides to go out to Kountz. He learns from another oil scout about a "redbone" named Turner. He goes to talk with him. The man expects to be paid a lot for a lease on his land, and Bo is interested at first. He talks to a geologist about checking the site for him, but he can't afford to pay the $100 fee the man wants. He settles for paying a Choctaw diviner $10. The diviner says there is no oil there and shows him how to distinguish marsh oil from rock oil. He decides to pass on the lease since he is not sure.

Meanwhile, Loretta is losing confidence in De-Ridder oil. She begins to take commercial secretary classes. Beaumont is still booming. Two hundred fifty gushers have been drilled yielding over 60,000 barrels a day. Refineries are being built in Beaumont and Port Arthur. Ocean-going tankers are carrying Beaumont crude to the east coast. But still Loretta feels uneasy. Things are already changing. Sucker trains no longer arrive.

Bo goes to Sour Lake. A well has been started there. He suspects that it will produce oil. He sneaks into its slush pit at night and discovers oil in it. He finds an acre of land for sale for $1,000 and buys it. Then he has the difficult task of moving his rig to the site. He hires Purvis and his team of oxen for $100 to move the boiler. For the derrick, he has to buy lumber and have it shipped to the site. He has no money to pay to have the derrick erected, so his crew has to build it. They work with handsaws and crosscut saws in rain and sun. They cut palmetto fronds in the swamp to build two huts, each large enough for two cots. These huts keep out the daily rain. At night they light pine smudges to keep the mosquitoes back. They think of themselves "as thin as the razorback hogs that roamed the woods and mildewed to the bone." (FE 239)

He goes looking for more land to lease. It is not easy to travel through the Big Thicket: "Under-growth cut one year seemed heavier the next. It was good for deer and razorback hogs, the prowling bear and panther. It was hard on men and horses." (FE 239) When Bo returns from his scouting trip, he smells oil, Sour Lake's first well having gushed. Two days later Bo spuds in. Mr. Catell of The Double Trey Oil Company offers to buy Bo's well and land for $50,000. Bo and Shoemate decide not to sell. Soon Sour Lake is booming. But Bo hits a pocket of gas, and his drill string is destroyed. They will have to sell or start again. Catell offers them only $10,000. They refuse and start again after getting some cred-it. Bo still decides to look for new leases. He goes to Batson prairie and leases fifteen acres at one dollar per acre.

Bo and Shoemate bring in their well, and it's a gusher, but they find out that Catell has bought all the land around them and set up guards. They can't move any oil across his land without going to court, and they can't afford to go to court. They have to sell the land and well to Catell for $10,000, about what they have invested in it. They begin again, taking drilling jobs and soon are showing a profit. But on April 15, 1903, there is a horrendous fire at Spindletop, one which burns several whole tracts. Bo races to the scene, but there is nothing he can do. His rig there is completely destroyed.

This fire means the end of many Beaumont oil companies. DeRidder Oil is being sued, and fraud charges are brought against Hanrahan. He gets Loretta to put all of her savings, $3,000, into the company. She asks Bo to drill a well for them, just so it will look as if they really are a viable oil company. She believes that that will protect Hanrahan from the fraud charges. Bo looks at all their land and can find none that has a chance of oil. He refuses to drill a dummy well because it isn't honest. She tells him that she doesn't want to see him again if he won't help.

Hanrahan starts a saloon and brothel in Sour Lake and hides out to avoid prosecution. Loretta tracks him down. When she confronts him, he tells her that he is leaving for Mexico and offers to put her in charge of his place. She is offended and returns to Beaumont where she takes a low-paying job for a real estate company run by a drunken lout.

Meanwhile, in Sour Lake, there is a tragic incident when poison gas kills several people. Bo gets some gas but recovers. One of his crew is not so fortunate. Bo decides to wildcat at Batson Prairie. He has to blaze a trail through the thicket for the oxen team to drag the boiler. They can't use wheels. They cut down a tree and attach the boiler and "lizard" it across the ground and marsh. As before, they build their own derrick and live in palmetto-covered huts. Even before they can drill, they discover that they are a part of the wildest boom ever:

> There had never been a boom like Batson's Prairie. News of the discovery well brought men and women in a mad race. They came on horseback and on foot over the trail Bo had hacked out from Sour Lake. They came by train to Kountze from the north and east, to Liberty from the west, and then in wagons when they could hire passage, on foot when they could not. They forded bayous and bogged their way through marshes. Men and women, drawn from the cities by the fortunes to be made in oilfields, plunged into the wilderness of the Big Thicket, where water moccasins crawled, where nights were at times noisy with the roar of bull alligators. (FE 289)

There had been only five families living there, and then there were thousands. There was little law, one deputy sheriff. Bo sees a man shot simply for cussing someone.

Bo's well comes in "meek as a lamb." And he immediately begins developing his acreage before others can pump the oil from beneath it. He hires rigs and buys rigs and hires boll weevils to operate them. He has a house built right in the middle of the field, saying, "I am heap scareder of Fannin Street (downtown Batson) than I am of a oil well." (FE 298) They begin drilling in Saratoga. In Batson, they have three wells by the end of the year flowing 5,000 barrels a day.

Loretta, tired of her dead-end job and low pay, decides to set up as a public stenographer in Batson, little knowing what kind of wild place it is. She has to leave her typewriter and baggage in Liberty at the railroad depot and go on to Batson by wagon. When she arrives, she finds a place to stay and set up her business. But all night, people bang on her doors thinking she is a prostitute. She survives the night only to be arrested the next morning by the deputy sheriff for vagrancy. She is hauled in, protesting. Luckily, Bo has seen a box marked with her name at the railroad depot. He comes looking for her. But the only way he can get her released is to tell the deputy that they are married, a common practice for releasing prostitutes to some man's care. He professes his love for her, and she accepts him, and she is released. He pays her twelve dollar fine. Later he tells her, "I reckon I bought me a wife." (FE 333)

He offers to put her on a train and give her money, but he wants her to stay and be his wife. She agrees. On the application for a marriage license, she has to write her name, Gaither Ware. He is surprised, of course. She says Loretta Lee was her "roughneck" name. Preacher marries them, and they move into the house in the oilfield. There is no honeymoon because he has to go back to check a well which is ready to gush. On the way home, she sings the song she sang to him when she first saw him. They arrive at Batson, and she is scared by all the gas flares. She thinks the whole oilfield is afire. He assures her it isn't. Her married life begins in this field: ". . . they stood silently together for a moment and then blew out the coal-oil lamps. They could not shut out the flare lights that glowed rose-pink on white sheets, angry red on rough pine walls. They could not shut out the noises of the oilfield." (FE 340)

The marriage of Gaither and Hale is as traumatic as their romance. Hale is gone frequently supervising his operations in Sour Lake and Humble and even Jennings, Louisiana. She hates living in the oilfield and wants out. She becomes pregnant, and still Hale insists they stay near his wells. He becomes concerned that those who are gauging his storage tanks are stealing from him and prevails upon his wife to do the gauging for him. She does this, climbing daily almost to the last day of her pregnancy. The men in the oilfield are superstitious about having a woman working among them, but she goes about her duties in a very business-like manner allaying some of their worries.

Again, there is a poison gas tragedy. Hale is away. Gaither asks Preacher to leave the well he is drilling to bury one of the victims, and the well becomes sanded up and lost while he is gone. Hale gets on Preacher because he did as she asked him. Preacher responds, and Hale cusses him. Preacher quits and heads for the Jennings oilfield.

Hale has been to Humble on the day the baby is expected. He travels all night to be back on time but arrives only after the doctor is attending her. His son is born healthy, but Gaither is extremely weak. Hale asks the doctor to travel with them to the hospital in Beaumont. After a long trip over washboard roads, they reach the train station and finally the hospital. Gaither recovers, and Hale promises her that she will not have to return to the oilfield. He has bought her a house on Main Street in Houston, near some of the other new oil millionaires. She lives happily there for a short time.

Hale's most important well catches fire in Humble. After many attempts by others to put it out, Hale tries himself and is killed. Preacher comes to his funeral in San Augustine. Gaither, wondering about why Bo died and why he changed, asks Preacher:

> "Oil didn't burn him," Preacher said. "He burnt himself. A prophet warned us, if we'd a knowed how to read the warning. I couldn't help him, but I never carried a grudge against him. He was as good a man as e'er lived. We come to the oilfields together. I reckon you know that. We come up on each other on a road in the Big Thicket." He laughed, recollecting. "He was barefooted. We went it together a long time, till something happened to him. As I see it, he got to wanting too much. It wasn't you. It wasn't me. It wasn't oil even." (FE 384)

She says she still doesn't understand. He says, "It ain't given us to know how a man's feet are set." (FE 384) But all the way through the novel, the emphasis is on the bad decisions that greedy men make whether spouting oil to sell stock or drilling too close or any of many bad decisions. These oil men aren't fated to be destroyed. They make decisions that lead to their destruction.

Owens' novel is a good solid work, with interesting characters. It is close to the generic oilfield novel, having the poor, uneducated, ambitious young man working hard and growing proficient at drilling, then finding oil, then building an oil empire. It, like many of the other generic oil novels, shows the central figure continuing to work excessively hard even after becoming wealthy and powerful. He gains the beautiful princess for his wife, only to discover that she comes from as humble a beginning as himself. Finally, like many other heroes of oilfield novels, he, though president of his company, chooses to go into the field and fight a well fire. His choosing to do so leads to his demise. Owens says in the end that it was Bo's choice that led to his death, not some evil inherent in the business of drilling for oil. *Fever in the Earth* is one of the better oilfield novels, full of interesting characters involved in every day oilfield work.

There is a clear description of place. The rank vegetation, the rains, the mud, the animals and the mosquitoes of the Big Thicket all play a significant part in the outcome, providing difficulties to be overcome for those who want to bring the oil from beneath the marsh.

Fever in the Earth is similar to novels written about the Eastern oilfields. Like it, they have explanations of the technology of drilling, have fires and explosions, have people with oil fever, and have boomtowns with prostitutes, swindlers, and gamblers.

Chapter 3

Big Thicket Boomtown

An earlier coastal oil novel, *Black Gold* (1950) by Jewel Gibson, shows us a boomtown on the edge of the Big Thicket, a vast marshy area North of Beaumont, an area still relatively impassible, full of dense undergrowth. Gibson knew oil towns well having lived in them with her husband, a driller. She sets her novel in Watson, obviously a fictional representation of the oil boomtown of Batson, which sprang up just as Spindletop was waning:

> Watson, Texas, that year of 1904 was a boom town, a wild town, whose breath reeked with alcohol and sulphureous gas. She was a loud town with a voice of innumerable steam whistles shrieking three times a day to the accompaniment of the never-ceasing rumble of machinery. She was a tricky town, promising riches to the obscurest newcomer and snatching money from the pockets of the most seasoned prospectors; shaking up the proverbial rich man, poor man, beggar man, thief, and changing their roles in the instant of a gushing oil well. She was a gay town, staying awake all night to lure men to her gambling tables and to her boom women, knowing that when the men got too rowdy, they'd be locked up in the twelve-by-fourteen holdover jail or chained to trees in the jail-house yard. On the surface she

was a community of towering oil derricks, false fronts and rutted wagon trails. Main Street itself was nothing more than the Madison Road gone wide so the wagons could whip around each other to the oilfield. In dry weather the street was passive, giving up great, dark clouds of dust to the feet of work animals or to the broad wheels of boiler wagons. But in wet weather it became a living thing, grasping with greedy black lips at the hubs of wheels and the bellies of oxen struggling under the threat of a bull-driver's whip. (BG 3-4)

The author provides a typical boomtown description of the central area of Watson but then adds information usually not recorded in these novels, what people said when someone died there:

As a rule, even a violent death in Watson meant little to the ordinary boomer. Or if a boomer were affected by a tragic occurrence, he hid his emotions under the protective coloring of such remarks as, "Well, old Hambone tried to guzzle up the slush pit today when the well caved in, but he choked to death on the mud." Or, "Fatty Higgins fell from the finger board last night and splattered up a brand-new derrick floor. You could smell Dixie Pale Beer for a hundred feet around." (BG 4)

The town is believable even if a little exaggerated. The characters are nearly all exaggerated, too. They are either eccentric, larger than life caricatures, or they are too pure, too good. One of the important secondary characters, Buck Trammel, is introduced first. He is "a wiry, sinewy man," a team-ing contractor. He is seen "staggering down Main Street; his shoes on the wrong feet as usual; his bottle in the pocket of a black rain slicker that threatened to slide off his shoulders to the boardwalk." (*BG* 4) Buck is often drunk from moonshine made in the Big Thicket. As he moves down the street, roaring drunk, someone tries to hire him for a job, and he responds, "Move you two rigs. Move you three rigs. You boys quit pushing me round on this sidewalk. Move the whole dal oilfield for you. Got the best dal horses and mules in the oilfield. Look at that black cat a-coming off that sign at me, Shorty." (*BG* 5) Every time Buck speaks he says "dal" something or other, his version of "damn." It gets "dal" tiresome before the novel ends.

We soon learn from Buck that he is going to a funeral for a prostitute, Alice Chalmers, who has been killed by "old Bill," an oil worker. Red Dillon, Alice's former boy friend, is making the arrangements for the funeral. Her son, Bass Chalmers, has arrived for it from Galveston. Bass, the protagonist, is too good and innocent to be believable. So also is Gloria Smothers, whom Bass meets. Gloria is the daughter of another prostitute, but Buck tells the reader what a good-hearted, pure girl she is.

None of the other characters are quite as nice and virtuous as Bass and Gloria, but they nearly all have good hearts. The evil character in the novel is the county attorney, Sam Graham. Sam and Alice Chalmers have been running a scam on Red Dillon. Alice and Sam had bought some oil land from an old mentally retarded man, Ike Hanks. They then got Ike to lease his land to Red Dillon. The scheme was to keep Red from knowing that the lease is not legal until after he has spent his money on drilling it. Alice has felt little regret for her duplicity: "Well, it's done, Sam. Red didn't even go to Linden today. My deed will be filed and forgotten about before he ever drops round to the clerk's office. He'll dig the wells for me. Me and you'll split the difference, and I reckon I ought to feel bad. Old Red's been damn swell to me. This will bust him" (BG 47)

After the death of Alice, Sam Graham has to figure out a way to make the scheme work. He finagles Bass into appointing him as Bass' guardian. Bass knows nothing about any of Sam's tricks and schemes. He meets Gloria, becomes interested in her, and decides to remain in town. Bass has taken an instant dislike to Red Dillon because he had been his mother's favorite. Red wants to help Bass, and he arranges for Buck to hire Bass as a helper. Bass takes a room in Mrs. Kooney's boarding house. Mrs. Kooney is another of the larger than life characters. She is outspoken. Unfortunately, she says, "Sy God," for "by God" even more often than Buck says "dal."

Bass goes to work as a swamper, and he is told how to keep the mules working: "'To see that the swing team and the point team don't play off in no bog holes. The first time they play off, you swamp them in the ribs with the rings. The next time they play off, just rattle at them, like this,' said Shadow, taking the rings and jingling them." (BG 68-9)

But Bass' main job is jumping off the wagon and

clearing the road of trees and stumps — hard work. Before the day is over, he and Shadow, the mule-skinner, have a confrontation. Here Bass exhibits his stubbornness. Ultimately he and Shadow come to an accommodation. He learns his job, but it is obvious to Shadow that Bass doesn't have sufficient interest in the job to ever be a proficient muleskinner. In fact not long after he starts driving a team of his own, one of the mules drowns in the mud on the road. Buck Trammel can never forgive Bass for what Buck considers carelessness. Buck fires him and thereafter calls him "the mule killer." Before he is fired, Bass makes friends with Mack Martin, a lazy, conman. Mack quits work when Bass is fired. He says he left because he was standing up for Bass. He moves into Mrs. Kooney's boarding house. About this time, Gloria runs off from her mother's bawdy house and begins living at Mrs. Kooney's, too. Mack begins to court her in competition with Bass. One of Mack's ploys to get in good with Gloria is to bring her baby animals he finds during his frequent trips into the Big Thicket.

Bass is hired as a roughneck by Shouting Sandy, a driller for Red Dillon. He will be working on the crew which is drilling the Ike Hank's land. On Bass's crew are an old man and a sick man. For them, Red Dillon shows great concern. When Dillon sees Marty cough up blood, he says, "When the first damn bubble of oil appears on the slush pit, Marty, I want you to go home and pack up your duds. That Goddamn consumption's going to get you unless you go out west and get it cured. By God, I'll pay your expenses and you can take your family along with you. And as soon as you get well you can pay me back roughneck-ing." (BG 150-1)

Bass, like most of the young generic heroes of oilfield novels, soon discovers his strong desire to be a driller, and the members of Bass' crew see pretty quickly that Bass has brake fever: "And, let a man with the fever feel the old brake quiver in his hand, and damn, he was all done for. A natural-born driller couldn't any more resist a rig than an old salt could resist the sea." (BG 153)

While this well is being spudded in, Gibson pro-vides a detailed description. Part of this is a clear explanation of removing the pipe from the hole. Red Dillon figures out some ways to improve drill-ing by catching the drilling mud in a bucket and by using the rotary to break down pipe. The drilling goes well, and Red gets a gusher. He arranges with a company to ship and sell his oil, but he discov-ers he is not getting a check for payment. Then he learns of the tangled web woven by Alice Chalmers and Sam Graham. He thinks Bass is a part of the scheme and fires him. He then brings suit against Graham and Bass.

Bass gets a job as a driller for another producer based on the recommendation of Shouting Sandy. The other producer and Bass hire a detective to try to find Ike Hanks. Hanks, believing he was wanted for murder, had been scared off by Sam Graham. Bass finds him and gets him to testify even though it is against Bass' side of the case. Much of the last part of the novel deals with the case. In the end, right wins out. Graham resigns and leaves town. Red gets his lease and wells back. Bass marries Gloria. Mrs. Kooney gets the last word in the book when she tells Red Dillon: "Sy God, honey, don't stay down here all night. Me and you have got some talking to do. I'm a-feeling it in my bones, honey. The old bubble's getting ready to bust. And when it does, we want to make a run for it. Sy God, we want to hit the next boom town before all the good squatting places are took." (BG 329) So the novel closes by emphasizing the temporary nature of these boom towns. This is a good novel at showing the lifestyle of an oil town, and it provides an example of a young man who comes to the oilfield and becomes more enamored with oilfield work than with getting rich.

Chapter 4

Wanderers

In Mary King's *Quincie Bolliver* (1941), we get an exquisitely realistic picture of the Texas coast. Few people know this novel. Until recently it has been out of print, but it is superb and deserving of a high place in American literature. One of its best features is the numerous day-to-day accounts of the weather and plants and animals.

The protagonist of the novel is Quincie Bolliver. At twelve, she is brought to the Good Union oilfield by her itinerant father. Good Union is a small field, in the early twenties just beyond its peak period. It is eighteen miles from the Gulf of Mexico, near the mouth of the Brazos River. Mary King had been a child in a similar field during those years. Her father was a driller. On the cover of the Texas Tech University facsimile edition, there is a picture of her as a child, holding a kitten in front of oil derricks.

Quincie has never stayed in a place for long. Her father, Curtin, is a mule skinner and peddler, and he has kept her moving. Upon arriving in Good Union, Quincie and Curtin temporarily find lodging in Judith Paradise's boarding house. Judith thinks she recognizes their type: "The town had been full of their kind, the kind who lived in tents and flung their wash water through the open fly without bothering to step outside. They had come in wagons, in trucks, and on foot:

whole families and broken pieces of families."*(QB 12-3)*

Judith puts her to work to earn her food. Quincie uses this opportunity to begin to belong.

> A dozen trips made between dining-room and kitchen, and Quincie began to feel more at home. As she came and went between the two rooms, she talked to herself as she often did. "I been here a long time. There's two windows on one side and three on the other, with a door to the hall. In the kitchen there's two doors, one to the hall and one to the back porch. I been out there. I could get away easy if anybody chased me. There's a grease spot by that chair. That spot on that window screen looks like a goose stretching up his neck for corn." (QB 17)

But new people come in, causing her to feel once again a stranger: "The structure of familiarity she had taken such pains to erect crumbled about her ears. The house was again menacing with newness." (QB 18) She comes to live in this house under the live oaks and temporarily has a place, a place touched by the oil-field, full of clutter. The oilfield even affects the games she plays with Ellie, Judith's daughter. They dig with spoons in the sand. Ellie says, "Down a thousand feet, goin' though shale!" She responds, "Down two thousand!" Ellie comes back, "Three thousand!" She finishes, "Down a million! I can see oil now, Ellie, come look!" (QB 31)

Earlier it would have been easy for Curtin Bolliver to get a job in the oilfield, but jobs are fewer now, and he is not even able to catch on as a mule skinner. He works around the rooming house at odd jobs to pay for their board. Quincie sleeps with Ellie, and he sleeps in the mosquito-infested shed.

Judith has made money in the boom, but she has lost most of it in worthless oil stocks. She supports herself now by housing and feeding oil workers. One of the roomers is Nat Patch. Nat is fifty-five and is labeled "the old man." He has been a driller but is now reduced to firing boilers at a pump station because of his age. He dyes his hair to keep Cockerel Oil's management from thinking of him as old, but his ploy doesn't work very well as he is later demoted to a handyman's job, painting and repairing. One of the frequent boarders is the driller, Tip Morgan. He teases Quincie, and she doesn't like him and tells Ellie: "He's ugly. He's got hair like a horse's tail." (QB 46)

Quincie, in her desire for a place, is interested in the concept of property. Each room in the boarding house is like each roomer's property. Quincie worries Ellie with repeated questions about ownership:

> "Who owns all the derricks?"
> "The Cockerel Company, I guess."
> "And all the land, too?"
> "I guess so. I don't know."
> "Who owns that tree outside your mama's yard? I bet your mama don't own it because it ain't in her yard."
> "She don't have to own it—it just grows there."
> "Who owns the road? I bet the road don't belong to anybody." (QB 47)

While she is living in the boarding house, Ellie points out to her the Mexican prostitute. This is a different type of person than the working girls of most oilfield novels:

> The boom of two years before had been like a tide sweeping into the town. With it had come much drift. The greater part of this drift had ebbed out with the tide's passing, but the Mexican woman had remained. Like a small tree uprooted and carried along by a force too urgent to withstand, its branches finally swinging crosswise catching on the forks of other lives, so she had caught and come to rest in Good Union. She had come with a driller who had gone away with another woman. Because she could think of nothing else to do, she had stayed. She did not join her own people. The crowded section house, swarming with dogs and children, sent her no call she cared to answer. (QB 48-9)

Like this passage, some of the story is told from an objective narrator's perspective, but much more is through Quincie's. And hers is remarkable for her alert senses. Ellie notices that Quincie likes to smell things:

> "You all time smelling things," she said disgustedly. "Ain't you got no manners? It ain't polite to smell."
> "I wasn't neither."
> "You were too. I seen you. All the time sniffin' and sniffin' like a puppy dog!" (QB 51-2)

This starts an argument, ending with Quincie running off from the house and catching a ride to the oilfield in search of her father. She rides with a friendly mule skinner and finds out that there probably is a job for her father with his company.

When she reaches the oilfield, she sees a pump and describes it: "Slowly and strongly the beam moved — up, down; up, down. From its rising and falling head, a rod drove through the derrick floor like the beak of an insect plunging and sucking, withdrawing, plunging again. All around her, Quincie saw the giant insects drinking." (QB 57) Then the driver explains to her how the pump works. To Quincie, his explanation seems unintelligible. She and the driver talk about how the pipelines run all around underground all over the world. She compares the oil to blood, and he launches into an explanation of the kind of oil they are getting from this field, a heavy one with an asphalt base. Then we get a view of the oilfield through her poetic sensibility:

> Around them was a field of lights. Each derrick had a string of lights from floor to crown block, the nearer lights disclosing through the shadowy cross-timbers the black oblongs of racked pipe and the small forked bodies of men. Here the earth had no covering; it was bare and trampled, chaotic, humming with the red glow of fires and the sharp, white hiss of steam. Quincie had a confused impression of slow shapes, dark and heavy, moving close upon the earth, of pipes and tanks, of ditches, of fire reflected redly in a ditch. She saw the steep sides of another earthen reservoir. Farther away, across the field, only lights were visible: the small globes like ripe melons along a vine swung down from the sky. (QB 59)

Next, she is told that this is the field. And she thinks:

"But it wasn't a field. A field was an open place with grass. She saw no grass, no trees. Earth and steel and fire she knew, and the shape of a man and a mule, but she had never seen all these things together at night, and never completely alone as she was seeing them now. The field looked like hell in the Bible." (QB 61)

Failing to find her father, she returns to the boarding house. There she finds Judith in the act of throwing out a family of roomers because the parents, Fern and Clay Pollock, have again been drunk and arguing. Still angry, Judith sees Quincie and throws her out, too. Quincie and her father leave with the Pollocks. They find small neighboring houses to rent. Quincie tells her father about the job she has found for him. He doesn't think that is the way a man should get a job, but he does take it.

Quincie is glad to leave the Paradise boarding house, and for a while she is the mistress of her own little house with its own natural setting. Her father tells her about the nearby ocean, and she wants to go there. The oil men come to visit her father and talk about another mystery — what's below the earth, and Nat Patch worries about waste:

> What's down there? We're drilling deeper all the time, men studying all the time, finding out more about the past, making better drilling tools, better machinery, but when you come to think about it, we ain't done nothing but scratch the top. What lies under there that man could use? And the waste man makes of what he does find! Look at all the oil drained off in that slush pond! Whyn't they do something with it? That's fuel, that's time and money wasted! (QB 103)

Curtin says he wishes he hadn't wasted most of his life. When Tip laughs at him, Nat says he is too young to understand:

> "A man's a wastrel, a fool! He learns too slow, and the trouble is that his children coming after him don't start where he left off. They forget what he took so long to find out, the things he learned them. It ain't so! they say. They got to find out for theirselves. They got to start all over again from scratch, and all the time they got less to work with— the forests cut down, the coal dug out and burned. Where's more coal coming from when all the forests is gone? Time will see this earth we live on as bald as an egg, and the winds and the rains will come, and with nothing to shelter him, man will be washed into the sea."
>
> "You worry too much about waste," Curtin said. "We got a rich land." He motioned to Quincie for a stick of wood to mend the fire. "A rich land," he repeated. "I say you worry too much about waste."
>
> "Time somebody worried." (*QB* 103-4)

This is the most straightforward discussion of waste in the oilfield of any novel I have read.

One direct effect of the oil pollution is dramatized a short time later. The narrator first reports on the frequent flights of ducks. The narrator stops to talk about how their passage affects several characters then continues:

> A little way beyond, they saw the gleam of another pond. Once more the tired flock settled.
> They wallowed on the oily surface of the Slop

Bowl. They tried to rise. Feet churned the surface; wings labored. The strong wings that had never before failed to grip the air and hurl them upward and away from danger, the wildly beating wings failed them now. They were glued with oil.

Some of the ducks, by sheer momentum, rose a few feet into the air, flapped, and fell back, sinking deeper, their watertight body feathers no armor against the brown insidious penetration of the oil.

The pond churned with trapped and drowning ducks. Before long it was still. (*QB* 116)

Quincie and some of her neighbors go to see the ducks: "The Slop Bowl lapped in slow, heavy ripples against its south bank. Quincie saw limp stretched necks and webbed feet; bedraggled bodies, half-submerged and strangely thin." (*QB* 117) Two women argue over what kind of ducks they are. The son of one finds a live one and the mother tells him to wring its neck, for he "ain't no good to eat." (*QB* 117) The parents argue some more while the boy stares at the duck his mother wants killed. Quincie observes the women: "They were brown women, as brown as oil, some of them. Or maybe their faces looked dark and drawn because the sky behind their heads was so clear and bright." (*QB* 117) The mother tells the boy again to wring the duck's neck so that they can go home. Another flock of ducks sends the boy into action:

Just then a clear wild call came down to them. Another flock of ducks was passing over. All faces turned skyward. A grimace of pain wrinkled the boy's face. Savagely he grabbed up the bedraggled duck on the ground that had been trying weakly to clean its feathers. He held it by the head. Once, twice, he swung the body. The head parted from the neck like a ripe fig from its stem. He threw the oily fragment to the ground, slashed his hands down over his pants-legs to clean them, and whirled and bounded away. Quincie had seen tears on his face.

She hated oil. (QB 118)

Quincie tries to escape the oil by taking walks in the woods: "The air in the woods was heady and clean after the oil smells and the mule smells." (QB 122) One day she sees a freshly dug trench and thinks it is like a grave. Again, she compares oil to blood "The oil was like slow brown blood, the earth's blood. It was cased in iron and draining away. The world waited to gobble it." (QB 122)

Quincie and the neighbor, Fern Pollock, go to the movie and leave Fern's children locked in the small house. While they are away, the children play with the gas stove, catch the house on fire, and are burned to death. Fern and Clay are grief stricken even though Fern never wanted children and was not a good mother. Quincie is left alone, lonely, in her small inadequate house. Curtin brings Ellie to visit, and Quincie learns that Curtin and Judith are considering marriage. When Judith comes to cook a meal for Curtin, Quincie escapes to her woods, feeling as if her place has been invaded by Judith. She watches the heron fishing. Sitting in the rain, she thinks: "The house was Judith's now. She thought with shame of the grease spots by the stove, of one of her patched dresses drying on the line." (QB 133)

This is an important time for her as she works out

her feelings about Curtin, Judith, and her place with them. She finally comes to an insight:

> Her grief was wide, touching the still trees, the wet coats of the grazing cattle, the lonely posts of the power line, the soft feathers of the heron. Her pity was for all things: for the leaf set spinning by the rain, for the drops of rain that fell and were lost, for the darkening sky itself, and for the tender earth that must lie forever open to the sky, racked to preserve the running heel- and toe-print of all who chose to pass.
>
> The water in the ditch was only knee-deep. Without removing her shoes and stockings, she waded across and went on. Her terror was gone. She would never be afraid of the woods again. She felt as if she would never be afraid of anything. (QB 133)

She goes to live in the Paradise boarding house after Curtin and Judith marry. She grows up, feeling all the uncertainties of a young woman. She falls in love with Tyson, the Cockerel geologist, who rooms with them. She and he kiss, and he seems to be serious about her, but he is a selfish philanderer, and he starts romancing Ellie, who is attending school in a nearby town. Meanwhile, Tip Morgan has had an affair with Fern Pollock, and Clay Pollock discovers it. They manage to avoid the fight that everyone expects until they are thrown together while fighting an oilfield fire. Clay stops fighting the fire in order to attack Tip. They are seriously injured and burned before the extended fight ends. Clay and Fern move away.

Quincie takes up with a local grocery boy after Tyson leaves, but she is still in love with Tyson. Finally,

Tip shows an interest in her. She has sworn not to marry an oil man because she doesn't want to be traveling around again. Tip owns land, and she hears him say that he is considering leaving the oil business in order to farm his land again. Tip invites Nat, Curtin, and Quincie to visit his farm. When the time comes to go to the farm, Curtin doesn't show. Probably he isn't there because he is seeing the Mexican woman on the side because he and Judith have not been sleeping together for several years.

Tip shows Quincie the farm, and she is taken with it:

> Quincie followed the men around the house. Gate and house and path and barn were well known to her in some dream from the past. She had been here before, she thought. She knew that this was not true, and yet the idea persisted. Her feet seemed to know the ground.
>
> While Tip talked with the negro inside the barn, she sat on the woodpile and looked about her. A willow tree grew beside the woodpile; in its rough crotch hung two field hoes. A turning-plow lay against the barn wall. Its blade, she thought, was like a bird's keen wing. She saw herself following it down a row. Words once spoken by her father came to her from the past: "My people was all farmers, and by rights I should of been a farmer too, only somehow I shook loose and never went back. Some people got land in their blood, but I reckon I took after my uncle Billy Whiteoak, and Uncle Billy had a itchy foot."
>
> She was one of those who had the love of land in their blood. She knew it now. (QB 316)

When Tip takes her in his arms, she is as attentive to the land as she is to him. Quincie and Tip are married after some wrangling over her affections for Tyson. She marries him because he has roots unlike most in the town who are leaving now that the field is drying up. Curtin, too, loses his job. He wants Judith to sell her house and move away with him. Judith refuses. She is rooted in Good Union.

Quincie discovers that she has miscalculated. Tip plans to move with his job: "Oil is my work. I'm a oil man. I ain't no farmer — not any more. I couldn't hold a plow in a furrow, and what's more, I don't want to. I had enough of that when I was a kid. Farming's all right for a man that ain't got enough sense to make a living any other way. Me, I got sense." (QB 417) She responds by telling him about her desire for a place: "I thought I'd live in my own house on my own land. I seen the way women have to live in oilfields. I heard 'em talk. They come from nowhere and anywhere, and they head in the same direction. I been like that. All my life I had to eat off'n other people's dishes. I want my own dishes." (QB 317)

Tip promises to build her a house and tells her she would be lonesome away from everyone. When she said she wouldn't, he repeats that he is an oil man, that she married an oil man. She responds that he is married to oil not her, ". . . stuck all over with oil like a fly on flypaper." (QB 4193) He say that she talks like a fool. She responds by saying that she wanted to raise bees. He walks ahead of her and tells her that she has to choose. He will not have a woman trailing after him, whining. He says what will it be, him or the land. He says that if she married him for the land she could have it: "You can go live on the goddam' farm if you want to, but you'll live there by yourself. You can have land, all right. Sure, you can have it!" He makes her choose, "Me or the land? Do you come with me, or do you stay?" (QB 419)

She runs off from him, and he doesn't follow. She feels sorry for herself, thinking of herself "as a small figure, abandoned and lonely." (QB 421) She finally comes to an understanding:

> She had done all this before. Maybe the new person she felt herself to be was not new at all. Maybe it had been living in her all along. She was not herself, but her mother and her father. Her mother had run away once, and her father had been running away all his life. (QB 422)

She continues toward home stopping only "to look at the shabby ghost of the derrick. Fireflies wove in and out of the sagging timbers." As she reaches town, she sees Curtin meet the Mexican woman and sees them leave town together. She feels lonely as she watches them go. She once again heads home, knowing that in a few days she will be leaving, too, with Tip. The novel's final two sentences are, "She knew how it would be. It would be all right." (QB 422) "All right" is not such a ringing endorsement for her marriage and her future. For a woman who wanted a place, her place, this life is not one which can be pleasant, even "all right."

Quincie Bolliver is an excellent novel with many believable characters. It has a rich, poetic texture. It brings Good Union to life. It raises some important issues — the waste of the oilfield, the vagabond life of those who move from oilfield to oilfield, the treatment of old workers, and the depression of those remaining in Good Union

Mary King's *Quincie Bolliver* is unlike any other oilfield novel. It is in no way generic. It is a superior work of fiction standing with the best of the twentieth century. It has believable characters, behaving in believable ways. It is both realistic and lyrical. It is one of the few oilfield novels with a female protagonist. Quincie, like Bass and Bo, has to make important decisions about her life. She would prefer a stable rooted life, not the itinerant one of those who follow the oilfield. Quincie is a remarkably sensitive, sensual individual, noticing the weather, winds, plants and animals — no other oilfield novel so graphically provides a sense of place.

Oil Novels
of
West
Texas

Chapter 5

Wildcatter In a Cowboy Hat

The earliest oil-field novel set in West Tex-as — *Tarrant of Tin Spout* (1922) by Henry Oy-en[1] — fittingly has a cowboy hero. Its hero, Spence Tarrant, has been a cowboy but is already an owner and producer of oil wells. None has been able to produce enough to make him wealthy. But he has not lost his skill as a cowboy as he demonstrates in one of the first scenes. In a herd of work horses be-ing unloaded in Tin Spout is, by mistake, a famous bucking horse. When the new owner of the herd threatens to shoot the horse because of his wild-ness, a pretty young girl steps forward, calls him a brute, and asks him if he really plans to destroy the "pony." He responds that it "ain't no pony. That's a devil in horsehide." When she counters, "He's a finer thing than you are," (*TTS* 15) the oilmen there shout in approval. Then she turns to them asking them to stop it. Tarrant tells Sam, the owner of the herd, to make the bronc his saddle horse. Sam re-sponds: "What? Me ride that wildcat with hoofs? Man, I ain't no rodeo performer. You take off that

---

[1] Oyen was a professional writer, churning out a book a year over several years. First he wrote about his native Wisconsin. Then *Country Gentleman* sent him to various parts of the country to dramatize life there. He published a novel about the Mississippi Valley and one about Louisiana before he came to Texas to write *Tarrant of Tin Spout*. He died suddenly of a cerebral hemorrhage before he could proofread it.

sombrero, Spence. You're an oilman. Where do you head in talking horse to me?" (*TTS* 17) Spence says that he wouldn't talk horse except to a horseman and that Sam shouldn't make a fuss about riding the little pony. Sam decides to bet Spence a hundred dollars that Spence can't ride him. Spence says that he used to ride horses, but not now. Pointing to Spence's cowboy hat, Sam said, "Put up or change your hat!" Spence, saying that he likes the style, refuses to take it off. Sam counters, "Tell you what I'll do, Spence: I'll bet the pinto against your hat. You got no business wearing that hat, fooling round oil." (*TTS* 16) Spence agrees to the bet. Then, the narrator comments on the change of the area to oil: "The skill with which the horse was thrown and saddled testified to the number of former riders among the oil workers. It was an oil country now, a land of industry, of machines, but only a few years ago the horse had been king there instead of gasoline, and the cult of the saddle horse still was strong." (*TTS* 16) Then the narrator describes the oilmen's propensity to gamble:

> They were oilmen, and therefore anything that might add a new fillip of excitement to their already tense lives was welcome; and anything that might be made a gambling proposition to supplement the great gamble of drilling for oil was doubly welcome. Operators, lease hounds, rough-necks and skinners shook money at one another and sought stakeholders. Chili Joe, proprietor of the Skinners' Rest eating house, ran out and began to hunt odds. (*TTS* 17)

When Tarrant climbs in the saddle, the crowd hollers, "Eeeeee-yow! Ri-i-ide 'im, cowboy!" (*TTS* 17) Of course, it isn't easy, but Tarrant rides the horse, and it becomes his faithful saddle horse. He immediately becomes enthralled by Marjorie Dickinson, the young train passenger who had defended the horse. Her father, Dr. Dickinson of Chicago, has a bad case of oil fever and has given up his practice and virtually everything else to chase oil riches. So far, he has only found a conman named Bodine. He has invested everything in Bodine's oil stocks. Bodine is trying to sew up the entire oilfield and to get everyone in Tin Spout and Rangers Falls to invest in his company. He is also trying to stop any drilling until he can get more money out of Eastern investors.

Bodine wants Spence Tarrant to quit drilling for fear that he will have dry holes and this will scare investors away. First he tries to stop Spence by sending Spence's friend and former partner, Wayne, to persuade him. Spence is not persuaded and tells Wayne a long tale about what the Kiowas had done to his grandfather that kept him from having oil fever:

> "Done what?" he demanded. "Scalped him?"
> "If it had only been that!" murmured Tarrant. "No, the old gent kept his hair, but he was out of luck just the same. You know, the Kiowas used to poison their war arrows in those days; used to dip 'em in a mixture their medicine man cooked up for them. My grandpop got away all right, but before he did those Kiowas had shot him so full

of war arrows he came riding home looking like a sage hen that had been caught in a cyclone. But that wasn't the real trouble. The Kiowa medicine man happened to have an off day that day and he didn't have any medicine ready, so he had the bucks dip their arrows in a black slush pool side of a little creek. Wayne, you could never guess what that slush was?"

"What was it?" asked Wayne impatiently.

"An oil seep!" cried Tarrant, slapping him boisterously on the back. "Man, they shot the old hombre so full of crude petroleum that it inoculated him and his whole darn family and rendered them immune to oil fever forever and ever!" *(TTS 11-3)*

Dr. Dickinson's oil fever becomes a major part of the plot because he is encouraging, even demanding, that his daughter marry Bodine, and he tells her to have nothing to do with Tarrant. She goes along with him even though she recognizes her father's weakness

Bodine tries to keep Spence from blasting his well by buying the company doing the torpedoing. Spence manages to get it done anyway but gets only moderate results. The well will produce enough to give him money to do his next wildcat.

Not knowing who he is talking to, Spence makes a pompous old fool the butt of one of his tall tales. The man keeps asking him how he knew where to drill. At first, Spence answers him seriously, but the gentleman keeps asking stupid questions. People gather around to hear the stories. Finally, Spence tells him a cock-and-bull story about being caught on top of a gusher for hours with people trying to rescue him with extension ladders. The old man finally asks him how he got down. Spence says that his good friend Elmer roped him, "just yanked me off that column of oil and broke my neck." (TTS 65) Everybody laughs at the old fool, who turns out to be Dr. Dickinson, Marjorie's father and now Spence's enemy.

Often in oil novels, the hero has a crochety old fellow who is his good friend. For Spence, Elmer is driller and sidekick. He is completely loyal to Spence and is as fearless and formidable as Spence. The two of them are threatened by Bodine's hired gun, Grogan. Tarrant rescues Marjorie by confronting and bluffing Grogan, doing it without a gun. After this Bodine starts playing rough. He burns Tarrant's wells and storage tanks. Tarrant retaliates by burning Bodine's. A tidal wave of burning oil burns down Tin Spout. Bodine uses the publicity from the fire to sell even more stock, and Tin Spout is rebuilt immediately larger than it was. The boom is for real.

Spence drills a wildcat down to where oil should be and then conceals what he discovers when he studies the cores. He goes to the oil exchange and offers to buy up all the outstanding shares of his well. Since he is willing to buy, Bodine starts buying and even buys Spence out, paying him $100,000 for the well. Spence sells it to him although he knows it is dry, and he uses the money for another wildcat, this one far from any other wells.

Tarrant has only one day to pick up his expiring lease on the Stringer ranch. Stringer is a former rancher and former boss of Tarrant. Stringer has struck it rich. He now owns the largest hotel in Ranger Falls. In order to pick up the lease option, Tarrant has to race Bodine, who has his powerful car. Tarrant wins the race by swimming his bronc through a rain-swollen river that has washed away all the bridges. He has only two months to complete a producing well, or he will lose his right to the entire lease. It comes down to the last day because of the usual problems of having to drill through rock and having the drill stem break. He even runs out of casing, but continues to drill, luckily it's through clay, and the well doesn't cave in.

The day before the deadline, he has gone beyond the depth at which oil would have been expected. He tells the crew to keep drilling while he goes into town to fight Grogan, Bodine's gunman. He draws his pistol in response to Grogan's challenge and wounds Grogan seriously. He is arrested by a local lawman, one of Bodine's henchman. Bodine lures Tarrant's crew into town by making them believe that there is a lynch mob attacking Tarrant. Then, Bodine burns Tarrant's derrick and drilling rig. When Tarrant's crew returns to the well, they decide to blast the well in hopes of bringing it in.

The next morning, Tarrant's lawyer gets him out on bail. When Tarrant gets out, he hears about the burning of his derrick and rig, so he goes to Bodine's office. They engage in a bodacious fist fight, which Tarrant wins. About this time, the sound of his well breaking loose comes from afar — the gusher has come in with forty minutes to spare. He will retain his lease. Tarrant lets Bodine up and says he can go, but a little man steps forward, an agent of the department of justice, and says, "He cannot. I want him for breaking the postal law." (TTS 295)

Tarrant turns immediately into a busy oil executive, giving instructions about catching the oil and capping the well. Soon afterwards, he and Marjorie clear up their misconceptions and are married. The novel ends here, so we don't know how they deal with all the oil wealth that will be theirs.

One other rancher and his wife are in the novel. Before they struck oil on their ranch, they were called the Deaf Heeps because they could never hear the people who came to collect money from them. And there were many because they were extremely poor. After they become rich, they don't know how to enjoy the wealth. They are so bored that they buy a rooming house to run. Mrs. Stringer, the other former ranch wife, is much more resourceful. She spends her money making herself beautiful so that Mr. Stringer won't start looking at younger women.

Though a cowboy, Tarrant is a generic hero of an oilfield novel, having started from humble beginnings and worked hard, and finally succeeded in attaining riches and a beautiful wife with the help of Elmer, his mentor and sidekick.

Chapter 6

Lawyer With Oil Fever

A rancher also appears in two scenes of William Gilkyson's *Oil* (1924), partially set in Deaf Smith County in West Texas. The old rancher, Bill Carhart, is sharped in a lease deal by the central figure of the novel, Hugh Warrick, a lawyer from Philadelphia. On a ship returning from Europe after World War I, Warrick, a colonel, meets, Imogen Marr, daughter of an oil man. She likes him and, even though she knows he is married, gets her father to hire him to do some title searching and oil leasing in West Texas. Her father, Henry Marr, and his partner, Mr. Seagrim, are similar to Bodine in that they form corporations and manipulate the stock in order to cheat the stock holders. They produce some oil, but they rake off most of the profits. Seagrim tells Warrick how to deal with the other scouts: "I never saw an oil scout yet that didn't like his whisky — you can learn more from a drink, sometimes, than you can from a geologist." *(O 40)*

Warrick is willing to do whatever is necessary to lease the land as cheaply as possible. He joins up with Bob Farguhar, a water-well driller and employee of Seagrim's. Warrick pretends to be looking for water investments. He lets Farquhar approach Carhart to try to lease his vast acreage at 50¢ an acre.

Much is made here of the rancher and his appearance. The narrator speaks of Carhart's "far-seeing eyes, deep in a network of wrinkles." And again he speaks of "misty far-seeing eyes," and a "ragged mustache." (O65) Farguhar does the bargaining first, offering 25¢ and guaranteeing to drill within six months. Carhart says that ranchers nearer Amarillo are getting ten dollars an acre. He says he will give them a lease at $1. They offer him 50¢, but he won't take it. He says McMenamin of 5 States Oil will give him a dollar an acre. So they can't make a deal initially. But Warrick knows that the rancher is land poor and needs the money badly. Warrick, the newcomer, begins to get oil fever: "A dry wind was blowing from the north; it sang in Warwick's ears with a low humming sound, like the tingling of countless nerves. The thought of oil, of that enormous power, lying passive beneath his feet, locked in still Stygian pools within the confines of the earth, stirred his imagination, kindled it into sudden flame." (O66) He then says to Farquhar, "Something gets into your blood down here," and "Gee, how I'd like to drill this land for oil!" (O68-9)

Warrick says that he has heard that oil is a mean game now and asks Farguhar if he knows Seagrim. Farguhar explains to Warrick how Marr and Seagrim cheat their investors. With Farquhar, Warrick visits his first well. The driller explains to him how things work. Afterwards, he gets a little philosophical about oil: "It took men to get oil — the energy of man to release the still silent energy below. An age-old need, that, to renew, to increase — the fable of Antaeus, always true. He wondered for a moment how far man was molded by the matter with which he dealt — how completely the substance could become the spirit. It was hard to say. Oil was curious stuff — mysterious as black magic." (076)

McMenamin, the 5 Star oil scout, knows whether or not his company has struck oil in a nearby mystery well, Masterson 3. Warrick plies him with whiskey and learns that indeed oil has been struck. He leaves McMenamin passed out and hurries to Carhart's ranch. He lies to the old man, telling him that Masterson 3 hit limestone and that the company was giving it up. He then completes the deal.

Warrick looks honest, but he is no better than his employers. He goes to Wichita Falls to meet with Seagrim and Marr and accepts shares in the land he leased. He boasts to Imogen Marr of how he got ahead of McMenamin by getting him drunk and of how he withheld the information about the well from Carhart. When Warrick goes into the Burkburnett field with Marr and sees a gusher, he is even more excited about the possibilities of oil wealth:

> Five thousand barrels! That was fifteen thousand dollars a day. An acre of such land was worth a million dollars. God, how rich these chaps must be! And it came so quickly! None of the wasting effort—the long desperate pull that he had always believed essential to the making of a fortune. A sudden struggle, quick, sharp, intense—a little knowledge, and some luck, and—above all—the gambler's courage. That was the main thing. You had it, or you hadn't. There was something stim-

ulating about a big risk—throwing everything into one pot, and winning or losing with a steady eye. It was a man's game. A great oil operator was as wily and courageous as any Homeric hero. He saw for an instant the black column, solid, smoky, veiled in the dull iridescent mist; it stood before his eyes a profound enigmatic symbol, charged with half-visioned dreams of power. He turned to Imogen. "My dear, I think I'm in this game for good." He hesitated, then gathered force. "I believe I'm meant for it!" (O 285)

Warrick tries to work with Marr in Mexico in an oil scheme, but in the end he is the one who is not wily enough. After his affair with Imogen, she and her father abandon him, leaving him to die in Mexico. Finally, he returns to consciousness, realizes that he has been "a cowardly, rotten fool," and finds his faithful wife by his side. Nothing more is said of the oil business, but it can be assumed that his oil fever is over and that he will return to the safer practice of law in Philadelphia.

Chapter 7

Booming Borger

In Jack Walker's extremely accurate portrayal of the oil business in West Texas, *Boomers Gold* (1978), ranchers and oilmen learn to accommodate each other. *Boomers Gold* has many of the characteristics of the generic oilfield novel, having a neophyte oilfield worker with a mentor to help him through the rough and tumble of life in the wild, new town of Borger in 1926-7. Interwoven with the plot, there are many short essays about life in Borger. The information provides good background and is not so extensive as to be obtrusive.

The young oilman, Kimball Z. Wingate ends up in Borger only through a misadventure. He is on his way to California to study law when he is attacked in a train station by Joe Shay, a savage bully. Joe, who hates blacks, is about to cut off the ear of a black railroad attendant when young Kim grabs his arm. So Joe shifts his attention to Kim. He puts his knife away and rams into Kim injuring his ribs. Then Deafy Jones, the mentor figure, rescues Kim by stepping in and hitting Joe on the head with his pistol-sized shotgun. In the fray Kimball loses a bag that contains all his money. In order to recover it, he gets off the train in Panhandle and takes the truck leaving for the oil camp. He is in great pain on the trip, but before he gets there, the truck breaks down, and he and Deafy or left behind. Kim recovers his bag but has no way to get back to the train. To make matters worse, Kim and Deafy are suddenly confronted by a West-Texas norther:

> Just as they came to the top, there was a faint puff of cool wind. Low in the north lay a deep blue color. It wasn't a cloud, but it seemed to be moving. They stood for a few moments watching the mass move closer. At first it seemed to move slowly but as it got nearer it increased its pace. As Kim and Deafy stood looking into the north, a wave of sharp, cold air hit them full in the face. In a matter of minutes, the temperature dropped from a very comfortable degree almost to freezing. It was an eerie, unreal thing. (BG 32)

Deafy and Kim are then given a ride by Blake Terrill and his new bride in their Stutz. Blake and Deafy have been enemies since Blake stole half interest in a drilling rig when they were partners. And Blake gouged Deafy's eye out in a fight. Blake would not have offered the ride if he had recognized Deafy, and Deafy would not have taken it if Kim had not been in such pain. Blake is your typical oil baron, hard working and hard living. He is with his latest wife, one the same age as his daughter Wendy. Wendy has grown up around oil camps but has been off to school in the east.

Deafy and Kim have to find a place to spend the night and get in out of the cold. After several disappointments, Deafy decides to take Kim to Sal's Place. Sal is a madam and a good friend of Deafy,

Wendy, and Blake. One of her prostitutes is gone, so the injured Kim sleeps in her room. Sal and Deafy sit up and drink and talk about old times.

Kim is still planning to go to law school, but he meets Wendy and is immediately smitten and decides to take a job as a tool dresser on Deafy's crew. Deafy is one of the best drillers around. He explains to Kim about the cable-tool rig. Soon, Kim is on the job, and he notices how carefully Deafy works:

> Deafy patiently showed Kim how to beat the point and flanges with a heavy sledge until it was sharp. Kim was impressed with the thoroughness of the work Deafy did. No matter how small or trivial the adjustment, Deafy did not leave it until everything was to his satisfaction. And, though Kim was anxious to get started, he knew that Deafy was really saving time by being so meticulous. (BG 96)

Next, the crew for the other tour is hired, but that leads to trouble when one of them takes down a wire holding in the horses from a nearby ranch. The ranchers show up wanting to be paid for two of their mares that died after drinking from a slush pit. The ranchers are an old man named Finch and a middle-aged woman named Mandy Beatenbow. Deafy makes the other tour's driller and toolie pay for the dead animals. He and Mandy are obviously interested in each other from this first meeting. Deafy begins riding with Finch, his new friend, to visit the ranch. The ranch matriarch is Granny Beatenbow, who has refused to lease the ranch for drilling even though Blake Terrill has tried to persuade her. He has taken Wendy along, and Wendy and Granny have become the best of friends.

The well that Kim and Deafy are drilling comes in a gusher. Deafy and Kim let Sal take care of most of their earnings because Borger is becoming an increasingly dangerous place since organized crime has moved in. Whole rigs have been stolen from drilling sites. Deafy again drinks with Sal while Kim goes looking for Wendy.

Kim goes to her house and is invited in even though her father has told the maid not to let anyone in while he is gone. Wendy has been a friend of Deafy since she was a child, and she tells Kim that Deafy's son was killed in the war. He thinks that that may be part of the reason that Deafy has been so good to him. When Blake returns and finds Kim there, he is angry. He has hired Joe Shay as his bodyguard and strong-arm man. Joe offers to throw Kim out. Wendy tells him that he couldn't. She fears and hates Joe. She carries a pistol and knows how to use it, and Joe knows she does. Maria, Blake's young wife, offers Kim a drink. He refuses and leaves.

Kim and Deafy have arranged to buy pistols to protect themselves. And they need them when they become tool pushers on the next lease. On one occasion, after picking up the payroll while Deafy is under the truck trying to get ice out of a fuel line, a highjacker sticks a pistol in Kim's ribs and demands the payroll. Kim doesn't have it. Deafy does. Kim delays the man. Deafy, seeing an opportunity, shoots the pistol from the man's hand. Deafy won't press charges, but he makes the bandit pay for the shell he used to shoot him. Deafy thinks that is the sort of detail people will remember and that he and Kim will be less likely to be held up again.

Wendy and Kim go for a picnic, and Wendy shows Kim a cottonwood oasis. She then takes him to visit the Beatenbows. She tells him: "You will love them. The whole Beatenbow clan lives on this river. There's the old grandmother whose husband homesteaded the place. And then there's Mandy who is Granny's daughter. She's a widow." (BG 154)

Kim and Granny hit it off quite well. He and Wendy grow closer and closer. She has decided to take a job as a teacher in the just-completed school. Kim agrees to take her to work on the first day. A drunken Joe Shay shows up with some of his cronies, and they try to disrupt the school. Kim steps in, and while Joe is telling his buddies what he is going to do to Kim, Kim hits him — hard. Joe rushes him again and takes him to the floor. Once again Joe is pulled off of him, this time by several men. Joe threatens him again. Kim has come a long way in maturity and strength since he has been working on the drilling crew, but he still is not eager to face the monstrous Joe Shay. But he is proud of the fight and can't wait to tell Deafy.

There are several other major scenes before the crisis is reached. Everyone goes to the Beatenbow ranch. While at the ranch, Granny says that Kim can drill a well on her small pasture if he wishes. He says that he isn't in the production business. She says that he might change his mind. He doesn't

even have to pay her anything until he has a producing well, and he doesn't have to sign any papers.
On the way home they are held up again. Then there
is a flood in which the payroll is almost lost, and
Finch is killed.

One day, Deafy and Kim are called in by Os-
chner, the supposed owner of the wells they have
been drilling. They are asked to sign a contract not
to work for anyone else. They refuse. Then Deafy
learns that he has really been working for Blake
Terrill all along. Though threatened, they quit their
jobs.

Kim and Deafy have enough money saved to put
together a rig and drill on the horse pasture, so they
decide to do it. Deafy puts his money up but refuses
to be a partner. He insists that Kim will be the boss.
They agree and start putting together a rig. Soon,
they are at work on their own well. Deafy surprises
Kim by telling him that Mandy and he are getting
married.

The Texas Rangers arrive in Borger to tame the
town. Soon they are moving all the riffraff out. Sal
is closed down and forced to leave. Deafy and Kim
find her and provide her a cabin to live in near their
lease. She and Kim have lots of time to talk, and she
tells him that Joe Shay is Blake Terrill's son, born to
a former mistress, but that Joe doesn't know it.

Deafy and Mandy are married at the Beatenbow
ranch. The guest include oil men and ranchers. After the wedding, Granny calls her sons in and tells
them that she wants to allow Blake Terrill to lease
her land because of the size of his operation and

his reputation for getting the oil out even under adverse conditions. That night she dies alone — just as she had wanted it.

Deafy is away on his honeymoon and then away because of the funeral, so Kim has to run the well alone because they can find no reliable help. Kim goes without sleep for more than seventy-two hours. He is almost delusional by the time Deafy returns.

Early one morning, Kim decides that he must get Wendy to marry him. He goes into town, wakes up the maid, and goes up to Wendy's room. Wendy talks with him but will not see him because she has "gas eye," a temporary inflammation of the eye caused by oilfield gases. He talks to her through the door, and she accepts his proposal. He goes away happy, having never seen her. Soon his well comes in. It's a gusher, but, just as in many other oil novels, it catches fire. He doesn't have money to pay an experienced oil-well firefighter, and even if he did, none could be there for several days. Deafy says he knows almost nothing about it because it is the first well that has ever fired on him in thirty years. It happens a lot more often than that at the end of oilfield novels.

Kim decides to put out the well himself. He goes to town to get the TNT and asbestos suits. There he hires two half-drunk men to help him. By the time they reach the site, the men have changed their mind. So Deafy and Kincaid, a friend and former employee of Terrill, agree to help Kim by training a hose of water on him and each other. The water helps keep him from burning up as he approaches the fire:

Then, with the mightiest effort of his life, Kim Wingate moved the heavy weight of the anvil forward and pushed it into the spewing flame that shot from the ground. He felt it fall and then jerk the TNT from his arm. Then he rolled backward and lay flat on the ground. Two seconds later, the well emitted a giant burp, and for a moment nothing came from the well. Then a column of greenish-black oil replaced the yellow tower of flame in the sky. *BG* 283)

As he finishes, the author describes cows watching him. That's a fitting West Texas end to the high point of the novel, which is soon over. Terrill's wife runs off with his crooked lawyer, and Terrill is unhappy about having to give her half of everything they have made since their marriage, particularly the Beatenbow lease. Joe Shay tries to kill a black man in the presence of the Texas Rangers. When he charges one of the rangers with a knife, they shoot him. Joe is buried on the same day Kim and Wendy are wed. Blake has not liked Kim but is finally persuaded to take part in the ceremony. Kim decides he has grown up enough to tackle the challenge he has always feared — medical school. Obviously, he hasn't caught oil fever. Wendy is happy about his decision. Blake and Deafy are reconciled, and Deafy will work for him drilling the Beatenbow lease.

This is another coming to maturity story with the young inexperienced man guided by his mentor. Gradually, the young man grows up, meets challenges, and succeeds — becomes a man.

Chapter 8

Two Cowboys

In Elmer Kelton's *Honor at Daybreak* (1991), two cowboys adjusts to life in an oil boomtown, Dave Buckalew and Slim McIntire. Buckalew, formerly a cowboy, is Sheriff of Caprock. He has been happy with the quiet town Caprock has been. Now with the oil boom, he has to deal with a severe crime problem with only one incompetent Barney Fife-like deputy.

Slim McIntire is a competent cowboy thrown into a strange environment. Ironically, Slim McIntire, who has lived all his life in West Texas, is suddenly a naïve outsider in his own country. As the novel begins, he is being driven into the boomtown of Caprock with its surrounding oilfield. When he sees the gas flares, he asks, "Is the whole oilfield afire?" He then says, "I'm glad I didn't doze off and just now wake up. I'd think I'd died and gone to hell." The talkative man who has given him a ride into Caprock responds: "You'd've thought hell if you'd been here a while back and seen that wildcat well burnin' out yonder a ways. Taken two men with it, it did. Snuffed 'em out just like that." (*HD* 13) Slim comes into the boomtown with little experience with the corruption of the world, having seen only Kansas City. The people who have come in from the outside, both the oilfield workers and the camp followers, are insiders, having been in other oil towns. These boomers have followed the gushers from place to place, many of them since Mexia and Spindletop at the turn of the century to Caprock in the mid-twenties. They are accustomed to the gambling, prostitution, and bootlegging — the price gouging, the holdups, the brawls, the cutting scrapes, the shootings, the general lawlessness.

Slim quickly discovers the dangers of walking innocently through an oilfield town. He is hit over the head, and his saddle, bedroll, and money are stolen. When the ranching job he has come to Caprock for is not available and he is without means of support, he begins to find out about the oil business. The Sheriff and Tracy Whitmore, later to be Slim's girl, discuss Slim. Tracy says:

> "I'd feed a stray pup that was lost and couldn't find its way home. He's got that look about him, like a lost pup."
>
> "He may not find his way home, but I have a notion he'll find a way to fit in wherever he's at."
>
> "He looks like a fish out of water around here."
>
> "There's a lot of us like that. Caprock used to be home to me. Now sometimes I feel like I've been dropped into a foreign country." (HD 63)

Slim innocently takes the first job offered him and begins work unknowingly with a man who torpedoes wells. Though it's highly dangerous, Slim does this for quite a while, gradually accustoming himself to the strange lifestyle. Then, his boss is killed in an explosion, and Slim is wounded. While he is rehabilitating, he works as a dishwasher at the cafe where Tracy serves. She is attacked by one of the gangsters running an extortion racket in the oil town. Slim defends her and is threatened by the gangsters. In encouraging him to leave town to avoid the revenge of the mob, Victor Underwood, a wildcatter, tells him, "This your first boomtown, Slim. You don't know about people like that. You don't know about Big Boy Daugherty and the men he keeps around him." (HD 244) So Slim leaves town and goes to work for Underwood. Underwood cannot pay him, but Slim goes in with several other outsiders working with this outsider of the oil business.

Underwood is the wildest of Wildcatters, drilling out on the fringe of the oil patch. He has had two dry holes nearby and is almost penniless. Slim works with three other outsiders on the oil well. One of these is Trinidad, an ironic outsider as the narrator explains:

> There was another point. Trinidad was Mexican, at least by blood. He had been born in Texas, as had his father and his grandfather, but whatever that might have meant in the eyes of the law, it meant little in the eyes of most other Texans. He was and always would be an outsider except within his own little group . . . an outsider, even a foreigner, despite the place of his birth. So far as he had seen in his limited observation of the Caprock oilfield, Mexicans had found little place, certainly not in the drilling crews. He had seen

a few building pipelines, which was crushing, backbreaking work, and he had seen a couple on a muleskinning job, handling the large teams sometimes required to pull equipment through the deep, clutching sands where even the heavy trucks could not always go. (*HD* 11)

Trinidad is out of work and willing to work for shares in the well. Another of the crew is Choctaw, a longtime employee of Underwood. He has a platonic love for Underwood's wife, Elise, and remains to work out of allegiance to her. He doesn't like cowboys but gradually warms to Slim.

The final member of this band of outsiders is Autie Whitmore, a drunk. Autie had been a highly proficient driller. But after a well exploded and killed his son, he has done little but drink until the group shanghais him to work with them.

Slim, like Kimball Wingate and Bo Carrington, becomes proficient at his job and thus a part of the oilfield:

> Slim McIntire was gratified at how quickly he learned the basic operation of a cabletool rig and the various tasks associated with it. He learned the difference between the bullwheel and the calfwheel, between the Sampson post and the headache post. He learned to fire the boiler and keep it running, to ram and sledge a new point onto a drill bit. He learned how to bail out the hole when the mud at the bottom became thick enough to impede the dropping of the bit, then run a bailer of fresh water to the bottom and release it without muddying the sides and risking a cave-in. He

learned how to set casing, its diameter decreasing as the hole deepened. (HD 299)

Slim has changed from his cowboy boots to work shoes, and his cowboy hat is smeared with oil. After the group make their strike, it appears that Slim is fully converted into an oil man: "He wiped his hands futilely upon his drenched trousers. 'How'll we ever wash all this stuff off of us?'" Choctaw tells him: "You never will. It soaks to the bone. You've got the mark on you now, cowboy, like a tattoo. I'll bet you never punch another cow the rest of your life." (HD 352)

Others are reaching an accommodation with oil and the oilmen. The old owner of the ranch where Underwood is drilling, Henry Stringfellow, says of Underwood and other decent oilmen, that they were "men to ride the river with." (HD 363)

All of these outsiders agree to stay with Underwood when he drills his next well. After the Sheriff is wounded, they and others decide to clear the town of the gangsters. They round the gangsters up group by group and ship them out. The gang leader is handed over to the Texas Rangers, also outsiders.

Elmer Kelton says in his author's note that his father and father's family were ranch people and that his mother's family was in the oil business. He grew up near Crane Texas, an oil town much like Caprock, so he is at least somewhat of an insider, and he paints an accurate picture of what life was like in a West Texas oil town. In one of his earlier novels, *The Man Who Rode Midnight* (1987), Kelton has the seventy-seven year old, Wes Hendrix, return briefly to see the ranch where he grew up, expecting it to be unchanged. Instead, when his grandson drives him in, he finds the remains of a worn-out oilfield:

> Jim Ed slowed and turned in. There was a cattleguard made of old secondhand pipe, and it had an oil company sign on it, with a lease name and number. Off to one side lay a small pile of rubble that Jim Ed realized had probably been Wes's father's entrance gate.
>
> Wes blinked, and sadness came into his voice. "Papa and us worked awful hard gettin' that gate to lookin' nice."
>
> The road was packed with caliche for the easier passage of oilfield equipment trucks. At intervals, abandoned oilwell locations lay like scars on the grassland, their pads sterile of vegetation because of the deep caliche and the oil spillage. Concrete foundations stood like tombstones to mark the death of dreams. Rusted pipe and twisted piles of heavy cable lay scattered like the battlefield relics of a lost war.
>
> Wes grumbled, "Wasn't none of that trash here in my time." (TMWRM 333)

The Man Who Rode Midnight could just as well have been called *The Man Who Loved His Land* or *The Man Who Loved Ranching*. Wes is like many of the other old men — faced with the difficulty of economic survival. In most of the oil novels, we don't see the kind of degradation of the land shown here.

Instead, we see ranchers able to keep their land and their way of life because of the income they get from leasing the land even when oil is not found there. But those who do have oil must become accustomed to a different way of life. Some adjust well like the Beatenbows of *Boomer's Gold*. Others adjust less well, like the Heeps of *Tarrant of Tinspout*. The young cowboys find it easier to adjust to the new ways. Spence Tarrant of *Tarrant of Tinspout*, and Slim McIntire of *Honor at Daybreak* like the oil work as well as its rewards. Similar to the novels of the other areas, those of West Texas still focus on leasing, drilling, producing, and financing. Even more than most areas, they feature stories of young ambitious men being tutored by veteran oil men, growing more competent and tougher, and attaining some success.

These cowmen who loved their land, young and old, are a part of the realistic picture of the west in the oilfield novels set there. In these novels are cows, cowboys, old ranchers, northers, and dust storms—and wide open spaces.

Chapter 9

Pipeliner to Producer

The Iron Orchard (1966) was written by Edmund Pendleton Van Zandt, Jr, a veteran of many parts of the oil business. He published his novels late in his life using the pseudonym, Tom Pendleton. *The Iron Orchard* is full of detailed information about many facets of the oil business. It is the first oil novel since *"646" and the Trouble Man* (1926) covering pipeline work in detail. The general history of the central figure, Jim McNeeley, is like that of several other protagonists of many oilfield novels. He begins as a poor, uneducated, ambitious young man, rises to great wealth through oil, then runs into difficulties because of his megalomaniacal desire to become ever richer.

Much of the first part of this novel is about the tough life that Jim McNeeley leads as a pipeliner. He comes to the job in an odd way. He is a boy from the wrong side of town who has been "presumptuous enough to try to court a girl from the higher stratum in the local caste system. "(IO 23) The father of his girl friend, Mazie Wales, uses his influence to get him a job with Bison Oil in order to get him away from his daughter. These are the depression days, and Jim, seeing no hopes with Mazie, takes the job. When he arrives, broke and cold in the Dead Lake oilfield, he is assigned to the pipeline crew of two sadists. One of them, Cap Bruner, the crew leader, likes to do his own hiring, and he tries to drive off anyone hired by the front office. (*IO* 23)

One of the best things about this book is the essay which precedes the narrative in each chapter. Most of these are detailed information about the history of and workings of the oil business, but one particular one describes the setting of the first part of this novel: "The land between the Colorado and the Pecos Rivers lies like a yellow dusty cowhide stretched on a Comanche drum. Burned dry by the white sun of summer and raked by the hot sandy winds of what in other climes is called spring and fall, it lives in a permanent condition of drought." (*IO* 23)

From this, he immediately leaps into the narrative, showing the travail of this neophyte pipeliner. By the fourth day on the pipeline crew, Jim is ready to quit. He lies exhausted on his bunk aching:

> Every muscle and tendon in his body ached deeply as though beaten and bruised and swollen with infection. Every attempt at movement drew an involuntary mutter of pain in his throat. This was the fourth night that he had been unable to drag himself to the showers or the mess hall, and this would be the fourth night that he would sleep in his grimy underclothes, his sweat-salted body unwashed, his matted hair uncombed, his belly empty. The primordial animal agony in his body occupied his entire consciousness like a dull red fire, ... (*IO* 35)

Then Pendleton shows us what makes him this way. After riding in the back of a freezing pickup, the crew is hollered at and threatened by Cap Bruner. Jim is put to work with Ort Cooley, his new friend, who tells him what to do:

> The weight of the steel pipe shocked him. It was a profound, dead force that seemed to be pulling him into the earth. Then he realized that he was expected to carry it across thirty yards of brushy ground to the gang, with only old Ort on the other end. He could scarcely believe it. With every muscle and tendon in a tight, quivering strain he heard Ort's tense command, "Step out!" and he set himself into compressed, wobble-legged motion. He soon realizes that he will be doing this same task, over and over all day, day after day. (1037)

Jim gets sick and almost quits, but another of his new friends, Dent Paxton, the bookkeeper, helps him get a warehouse job for one day, and he is able to rest over the weekend. He continues to be harassed by Cap Bruner, and the stabber, Buster Drum. Jim's first confrontation is with Drum. While working with him, Jim accidentally hits him with a rock thrown up by his shovel. Drum, a huge man, charges Jim in rage, pressing his glove into Jim's face while saying, "You hit me in the ass with one more little rock, hot-shot, an I'll pop yo' head like it was a flea 'tween my fingernails." (1049) Jim knows that he will have to stand up for himself or leave the job. It is "survival or ruin." He takes the handle from his pick and hits Drum in the head. At first, Jim thinks he has killed him, but Drum regains consciousness and comes after Jim. Jim hits him again and fears he has killed him, but Buster once again awakens. Jim threatens him, and after this he has no trouble with Buster.

Pendleton provides an extensive view of the life of the pipeline crew. Jim survives and after three and a half years becomes the most proficient member of the crew. He is the stabber:

> There was artistry in the way Jim McNeely worked now. He moved with an economy of motion that was graceful and sure. In his lean frame there resided a deep corded strength made of sound bone and tough sinews under perfect coordination. Not an ounce of strength was spent that was not needed. It took a good man to stab pipe all day long without relief. (IO 105

While Jim is working hard with the crew, a son of the vice president in charge of production is hired. Cap lets him goof off all the time, and he takes advantage of the situation. Most of the crew dislikes him, but Jim puts up with him, recognizing that such inequities reflect the way the world is. The young man, Clayton LeMayne III, called Pluto, works there only a short time. When he leaves, he says he will get Jim a job in the front office. Jim doesn't expect anything to come of it, and nothing does.

Jim makes his own way. He saves almost everything he earns, planning to invest in the oil business despite knowing what a gamble it is. He tries to prepare himself by spending his weekends going to drilling sites with one of the company geologists, Berry Wakely. They become good friends, and he tells Berry to let him know if he finds any great investment opportunities.

After catching the clap from his one adventure with a dance-hall girl in Tascosa, Jim stays away from Odessa, usually only going into Coker City, the nearby oil boomtown. While going there, he becomes attracted to Lee Montgomery, the wife of Clyde Montgomery, a company engineer. Lee is terribly unhappy with her husband and her life in company housing. Jim tries to seduce her, but she repulses him because she is married. She begins to fall in love with Jim, though. He is despondent following this attempt and goes back to his bunk house and gets drunk.

The next day, hung over and depressed, he has his final confrontation with Cap Bruner. Jim has accepted Cap's eternal cussing as long as it's not directed at him. But next day, Cap goes too far and calls him a "gold-bricking sonofabitch." (IO 159) Jim is so depressed that he doesn't fight him. Then Cap gives him the dirtiest job, one usually given to the newest man, taking the drain plate off the test tank and cleaning out the sediment. Jim is almost gassed. He manages to stumble out of the pipe and falls in a heap outside the tank. He passes out there. He is awakened by Cap kicking him and cussing him. He manages to clear his head enough to take a swing at Cap, and the long-awaited battle is joined. After a two-page fight, Jim has Cap before him still on his feet but dazed. Jim prepares a punch which may kill Cap. Then he stops, choosing not to, feeling cleaner and freer immediately.

Assuming he'll be fired, Jim quits the pipeline crew. As he is hitchhiking away, Lee Montgomery picks him up. She has decided to leave her husband for Jim. Thus ends part one, a graphic picture of life in a pipeline camp.

Soon, Lee is divorced; the two marry, and Jim begins a well-servicing business in Odessa. Jim is paying for equipment, so Lee takes a teaching job to help support the family. She also keeps the company's books. Jim is not satisfied with the slow way of getting ahead. He wants to get into oil production, where the big money is made.

He knows that under Coker City, near where he has worked is a pool of oil. The owner, an old cowboy, has threatened to shoot any lease broker who comes on his property. The major oil companies, having leases surrounding him, are quite willing to leave him alone and to pump the pool of oil dry from their nearby wells. Jim decides this is his best opportunity to get into the oil business, so he takes the chance of approaching the old rancher. The rancher is much like Carhart in *Oil*:

> A smallish man in dirty clothes and a sweated-out Stetson leaned against the rail fence of the horse lot, gazing at him, The man could have been on either side of sixty. He had the face of a half-demented chipmunk with small eyes deeply sunk in and too close together. He hadn't shaved

in days. The cracks running down from the corners of his mouth were filled with tobacco juice." (*IO* 188)

The old man doesn't say much when Jim starts making small talk. But he puckers and spits "a large brown-golden stream of tobacco juice which arced through the dry air and struck the dust a bare inch away from Jim McNeely's shoes." (*IO* 188) It is the tobacco chewer's insult.

As they talk, Coker continues to spit streams of tobacco at Jim's shoes. Jim finally asks for some Beechnut chewing tobacco. He then tells Coker that people in town are saying that Coker is a fool. Jim says he doesn't agree with them. Then he spits "inexpertly" at Coker's boots. He intends to hit close, but he spits on the boots and pants of the old man. Coker fires back. Jim tells him why they are saying he's a fool, tells him about how the big oil companies are pumping the oil from beneath his land. Coker says, "Sh-it to what they say." (*IO* 190) He then fires still another stream of tobacco juice.

Jim keeps talking leases, and the old man looks like he is going for his rifle, and Jim considers tackling him if he does. Then laughing, the old man says, "You the wuss goddamn t'baccer chewer ever I seed in my goddamn life! Who the hell ever told you you could chew t'baccer?" (*IO* 191) Jim says he didn't claim to be an expert at anything, "I'm just a pore boy tryin' to get along." (*IO* 192) So Jim gets the lease.

He will not pay lease money, but he will share the production with Coker fifty-fifty. Jim will use his biggest well-servicing rig to drill the 4000 foot well. It will be barely adequate for the task. He has no money to pay his crew. They agree to work for a double bonus out of the money from the first production. On thirty-days credit for the drilling mud, Jim drills the well. He gets his old friend Berry Wakely, the Bison Oil company geologist, to help him "pick the top of the San Andreas formation." (*IO* 195) And Jim gets his gusher:

> The hollow coughing became louder and more persistent. Then here she came, first a little trickle of drilling mud, kicking and spitting in dirty spurts, then a belching of mud, gas and oil and gravel, and then all at once a violent bursting forth from the pipe as from an awakened giant erupting in a pent-up antediluvian orgasm. A solid four-inch column of green-black oil shot powerfully from the pipe twenty feet across the slush pit, flowering at the end and splashing in a wave of golden green bubbles over the gray mud of the pit that sloshed up against the far earthen firewall. (*IO* 197)

Jim hires two of his friends from Bison, Ort Cooley as a night watchman and Dent Paxton as a bookkeeper. Soon a young inexperienced attorney, Jeff Dofflemyer, joins him. Jeff is of immediate assistance to Jim in landing another lease deal. There is a prime piece of oil land that has not been leased because the ownership of the land is being contested in court. Jeff suggests to Jim that the only way to solve the problem is to get a lease from both sides of the dispute. Jim jumps at the idea. He plans to get the leases and then market them to someone else. There are several interesting scenes as he negotiates a deal on the leases with Consul Petroleum. He bluffs Mr. Naylor, an executive for Consul, saying that he can drill the well himself if Consul doesn't make a deal with him. Naylor says that he doubts that Jim can even drill a posthole on that lease. Jim responds: "I can drill it. I'm just a small independent, but I can drill it, and I thought you might want a piece of the deal so you won't look like such a sap if I make a well." (IO 215) He is bluffing, and this is crucial for him if he is to be successful: "He knew that by selling his equity in the Coker City well and by hocking everything else that wasn't already mortgaged to the hilt, by stalling off suppliers and maybe pulling the Coker City rinky-do on wages again, he probably could drill this well." (IO 216) But he didn't like the odds:

> But if the Turpin well was dry, or a noncommercial dribbler—and when he faced the facts he knew that chances were good that is what it would be—he would be wiped out. Way in the hole. Probably have to go back to working for somebody on a salary. It just didn't add up There was no leverage in the deal that way. It was one roll of the dice—all or nothing—go for broke .(IO 216)

However, Consul comes through. Jim drives a hard bargain and gets the money to buy both sets of leases and a one sixteenth override. He also gets them to agree to employ him to drill the first well at the going rate. If it comes in a commercial well, he will be given all the other contracts to drill on the lease.

From these first two successes Jim builds a large company and a great fortune. He has many dry holes, and he misses out on a pool of oil in Scurry county, but he has many successes, too. Fifteen years pass, and he decides to return like a conquering hero to his home town of Winston.

Without telling Lee, he buys a large house, hires someone to redecorate it, and installs a complete staff. He plans a surprise party for Lee, bringing her in to her new house in a helicopter. As one would guess, she is terribly unhappy at the party and afterwards. There seems to be nothing of herself there, and she is expected to just be at her leisure, play cards, and entertain strangers at almost any hour.

Jim again sees Mazie, his old flame from high school. She is married now to Pluto LeMayne III, Jim's acquaintance from pipeline days. Pluto has become an alcoholic. Jim, himself, drinks heavily and spends money lavishly. Once, he even buys a Cadillac on his hotel bill. He has an airplane. In order to build his company even larger, he makes an agreement with some money men in New York. They leave him alone and let him run the operation pretty much as he wants.

Lee still loves Jim and hoping to make the most of a unhappy situation. When she returns early from a visit to her ailing father, she sees the door to the library open, and there she sees Jim and Mazie having sex. She pours a thermos jug of ice water on them. As she leaves the house forever, she says, "That's the only way to separate dogs." (IO 290)

Lee doesn't really want a divorce, but Jim makes only one attempt to talk to her. Their timing is off, and he leaves before she can forgive him. Shortly afterwards, they divorce. Then Mazie divorces Pluto, and Jim and Mazie marry. Mazie is even better at spending money than Jim. Soon she redecorates the house and runs up huge bills. Jim drinks and is not happy. Jim begins to lose his old friends as they see how he has changed. Jeff resigns after refusing to handle the divorce. Lee would take none of Jim's money, saying that he would need it all. She takes a job teaching in a junior high in San Saba. Ort Cooley gets drunk and accidentally shoots himself in his own booby trap.

Jim begins to run into financial difficulties. He needs to find a good lease to drill. He persuades honest Berry Wakefield into giving him Bison Oil's information. Berry at first resists, but because he has a mentally retarded child who needs special help, he agrees to give Jim the information he wants. Dent Paxton disapproves of Jim's attempts to corrupt Berry. So Jim fires Dent. Jim begins to drill on the disputed site, and Bison brings suit against him. His partners from New York try to stop him from drilling, but he pushes on by selling off parts of the well. Soon his empire is dependent on this one well. He works night and day, not even trying to sleep. Then, Dent Paxton commits suicide, and Jim has to borrow money to pay for the funeral. Whether from lack of sleep or from inattention because of his financial and personal worries, he lets the well get away from him. It blows out. When it does, a fire starts. Jim has to sell the rest of his interest in the well to bring in a fire-fighting crew. The only available crew is an old man, Al McKnight, and his nephew, Albert. Al directs Albert in how to place the charge. But the inexperienced Albert moves too slowly and is overcome by the heat. Jim goes into the fire after him:

> As he ran the glare struck into his eyes and narrowed them to slits. The heat—it was incredible—like opening the door of a furnace and forcing yourself into it. He felt the skin of his face pucker. The breath was sucked out of him and he could barely see the black lump of the tractor for the flaring jewel-like blaze. His hair began to curl and it felt as if his lashes were melting into his eyes. His limbs seemed to shrivel and lose power and he had decided he would never cover the remaining distance to the fallen man. Then he ran suddenly, headlong, into the rear of the tractor and fell down bruised and cut on top of the soft fallen form. The shape under him moved and groaned. (IO 366)

He reaches Albert and has to carry him from the fire: "He walked with the same over-burdened intensity of a young man many years ago, staggering under a deadening weight of pipe, determined not to go down." (IO 366) Then he manages to pull himself together to go back into the fire. He places the explosive, and the fire is blown out. He walks away straight into a tree and passes out.

The next scene and final chapter is in the hospital. Lee has arrived and learned that in addition to being burned, Jim has a massive coronary thrombosis. He is convinced that he is dying. She works to convince him to live. She stays with him through the night, and it seems in the end that he will live and that they will remarry.

The wheel of fortune plot of this novel is a common one. It is much like the Oklahoma oil novel, *Men Like Gods*, in plot and Jim McNeeley is much like its Bill Branning. *The Iron Orchard* is better than most oilfield novels both because of the basic information about the oil business and because of the depth of characterization.

Chapter 10

Bootlegger, Gambler, and Teamster

Unlike in the earlier West Texas oil novels, Clyde Ragsdale doesn't have any cowboys or old ranchers in *The Big Fist* (1946), but as in *Boomer's Gold* and *Honor At Daybreak,* he focuses on the lawlessness of the roaring twenties, the bootleggers and gamblers of the West Texas oilfield. *The Big Fist* is set in the fictional town of Maxim near the fictional town of Tawn Lake. These represent the Reagan County boomtowns of Best and Big Lake after the Santa Rita #1 discovery of May 28, 1923. Ragsdale gives us Sid Wittle's view of his father, Hosy Wittle, a bootlegger, gambler, and brawler. Hosy loves to fight and insists that his mild-mannered son be a brawler, too. The Wittles move to Maxim after Hosy breaks out of jail in Oklahoma. Hosy, who had been arrested for bootlegging, immediately goes into business in the oil boomtown. Twelve-year old Sid, reports the sights and sounds of a West Texas oil town from the mud of winter to the white alkali dust of summer:

> And on the still air, shot through with a heat that almost seemed to throb at a man's temples, the galaxy of sounds rising from the activities of the field went on with an unending rhythm. At

night the skies were tall, distant, and the stars were clear and bright. The lights on the rigs were strewn across the face of the earth as if thrown there by some giant, irresponsible hand, and the steam from the boilers floated up into the lights like veiled mists in some mysterious, enchanted land. But always there was the sound: the sound of labor; the sound that meant money. The bucking boilers, the hissing engines, and the deep-throated clanking of the mighty rotaries seeking the wealth clutched by Nature in the bowels of the earth. And above all the sounds was that of the mud-hog pumps with their rhythmic, methodical beats, vacuuming the muddy slime from the holes dumping it into constantly filling slush pits. (BF 87-8)

Wells are being dug throughout Maxim. Just outside the window of Sid's room, Burleson #18 is being drilled. Sid is awakened one morning at dawn by an odd roaring. "It was like a distant storm, subdued but powerful." (BF 89) He can hear men hollering and their cries are "like whispers against the great volume of sound." (BF 89) A gentle wind blows the oil onto his house "like a summer shower of rain." (BF 89)

When first arriving in Maxim, Hosy, as a cover for bootlegging, works for an oil company, but he begins paying off the sheriff and by 1925 has $25,000 in the bank. He runs his own gaming tables in his house. In 1925, after a flurry of new activity in the oilfield, Hosy finds something special to bet on. Carl Horner, a teamster, explains to Hosy about a new opportunity:

The oil company he was working for was expanding drilling operations and had given him thirty days to acquire and break in another team of boiler loaders, which normally could not be done inside of six months, even with good luck and a good team with which to start. With teams drawing down eighteen dollars a day, any kind of horse flesh was hard to get, much less a couple of animals that would have to be trained like circus performers. Used for loading the massive boilers weighing up to fifteen tons on the big eight-wheel wagons, such horses had to understand a man's voice and commands almost as though they were men themselves. If any trouble developed during the loading, such as a boiler snagging on the skids, the skinner often had to work on it in a position where he would be mangled or crushed if his team failed him. (BF105)

Carl knew where he could buy a pair of blue roans, weighing about sixteen hundred pounds each. One of them, Rock, probably would train easily. But the other, Rowdy, was nervous, even perhaps mean. Maybe Rowdy could be trained, maybe not.

Hosy encourages Carl to buy the team so that Hosy can bet Carl will succeed. Hosy puts up a total of $30,000 in bets on Carl. Several interesting scenes lead up to the moment of crisis when Carl's life is endangered. Carl has the difficult and dangerous task of loading a Lucy with his green team. A Lucy, a huge steel boiler, weighed ten tons. It has to be roped with chains and pulled up skids to the bed of the eight wheeler. The author describes the big moment when the skinner's life depends on the training he has given his horse, Rowdy:

"Hold! Hold! Hold!"

The roans responded. Rock edged forward, his neck arched and his teeth showing. Rowdy, uncertain, swayed aside. His neck bowed. He pawed the earth. He swung his head as if frightened, as if trying to locate Carl by the sound of his voice. Slowly, he began dropping back and Rock could not hold the great weight alone. Already Rock's hoofs were slipping. Foamed lather, mixed with dust, clung to Rowdy's body. It was all happening in split seconds and Carl's voice still came from beneath the boiler.

"Rowdy! Rowdy!"

Suddenly, it seemed for the first time, the big, troublesome roan understood what was expected of him. At the sound of Carl's voice, almost pleading, calling his name, he lowered his massive head. His hindquarters bore in, crouched, determined. The roans stood like blue-gray statues, holding the ten-ton weight with quivering muscles.

Carl came crawling from beneath the boiler on his hands and knees. He spoke again to the team and they leaned forward and with a groaning heave slid the Lucy up the remaining distance of the skids and onto the eight-wheeler. (BF110)

That big scene ends part one. After that, not much relates to the oilfield. Hosy grows extremely rich but begins to lose his memory, probably from drinking too much of his own product. He loses most of his money in the stock-market crash of 1929. Much of the plot concerns the conflicts between Hosy and his wife, Anna, particularly in regard to his jealousy of Anton Cromwell, Anna's former pastor. Anna dies during child birth. Hosy kills a policeman after being caught running tequila from Mexico. He later kills Anton Cromwell. He always manages to escape from jail. Maxim's oilfield plays out during the depression, and many of the people end up hoboing. Sid hoboes for a while and finally takes a job at a farm run by a cranky old man, who turns out to be his father. They reconcile.

This is one of my favorite novels about the oifield. It is in no way a generic oilfield novel but provides a good picture of life in Maxim and a great insight into the character of a young man with a dominant father.

Oil Novels
of
North Central
Texas

Chapter 11

Oil and the Banks

In the late teens and early twenties, the greatest oil booms were in North Central Texas — in Iowa Park and Burkburnett north of Wichita Falls and in Breckenridge, Ranger, and Desdemona south of it. Several novels and short stories tell the stories of these oilfields and boom towns. The owners of the lands on which the oil was found were not much different from many of those in West Texas, mostly poverty-stricken whites seeking to hold on to their small farms and ranches. Oil production from these fields extended into the Thirties and the depression, and often the wealthy lost everything as banks failed and oil prices plummeted. The authors of North Central Texas oilfield novels recorded as many fires, explosions, and accidents as those writing about other oilfields, and just as many young men matured through oilfield experience, but to an extraordinary degree, novelists wrote about banking and bankruptcy.

The first oil novel set in North Central Texas was *Flowing Gold* (1922) by Rex Beach[1]. To a reader today, it has the feel of an historical novel, but it was published only five years after the first wells were drilled in Ranger and Burkburnett and three years

---

[1] Beach (1877-1949) wrote many novels and short stories, from which forty-six movies were made from 1910-1955.

after the extension to the Burkburnett field, which it describes in some detail. It also was published only four years after the end of World War I, and Calvin Gray, the protagonist, seeks economic revenge for a wrong done to him by a fellow officer during that war. As the novel begins, Gray appears to be a con man. He dresses exceptionally well as he takes the best suite in the best hotel in Dallas, but he is penniless. He is articulate, suave, genuine — giving everyone the impression he is someone important. He meets bankers, the mayor, and other important Dallasites. Everyone assumes he has a large fortune, and he does nothing to dissuade them. He anonymously calls the newspaper and tells the reporter that the famous Calvin Gray is in town. The reporter writes the story Gray gives him, a tale of the many adventures he has had around the world.

A jeweler he has befriended, a Mr. Coverly, needs someone to take jewels out to a rich oilman near Ranger. Gray volunteers to do it saying that he doesn't need the money it's only for the recreation. He only asks Coverly for money to cover his expenses. A man named Mallow has been hanging about the jeweler. Gray decides that Mallow is up to some skullduggery, but he has no fear of him.

Soon Gray is on the way from Ranger to the farm of Gus Briskow, the oilman. Gray is being driven in a rented car by an obvious scoundrel provided by Mallow. When he arrives at the farm, he finds Mrs. Briskow and her daughter, Allegheny, hoeing in the garden. The daughter, nicknamed Allie, is a large, shapely young woman, completely ignorant of the world beyond their farm. Though they seem extremely crude to him, Gray sees their better qualities, particularly the sensitivity and intelligence of the girl, even as she is dressed in gingham and brogans.[2]

Gray shows the women the diamonds. Allie is so large that she can only wear a ring designed for a man. The price of the ring is high, but Gus is determined that his family will have the benefits of their new wealth even though they have just begun to see what they can do with it. He and his son, Ozark, called Buddy, arrive from the field. Soon the whole family becomes open admirers of Gray. Before Gray leaves for Ranger, he asks Granny for some cream.

On the way back, Mallow and another thug attempt to hijack Gray, but he foils them by throwing a poisonous substance in their eyes. They scream in pain. Gray provides cream as an antidote for the poison and then turns the pair over to the sheriff in Ranger. His exploits are written up in the Dallas newspaper, and Mr. Coverly is waiting for him upon his return to Dallas. He gives Gray a bonus for selling the diamonds and protecting them.

While visiting the Briskow farm, Gray has promised to take Mrs. Briskow and Allie shopping for appropriate attire. They arrive in Dallas wearing the most outlandishly inappropriate clothes possible, and he is able to help them only with the outer clothes. When he asks for help on the undergarments from a salesclerk, she is rude and condescending. A young attractive woman comes to his

_____

[2] The Briskow family seems to be the models for the TV sitcom, *The Beverly Hillbillies*.

aid. She calls herself Miss Good. And she will tell Gray nothing of herself even though he is quite interested. Following the makeover, Allie comes out looking absolutely stunning, but she remains overly self-conscious about how she looks and behaves.

Gus Briskow comes to Dallas and offers Gray an opportunity to buy an oil lease, one on which the option will expire the next day. It's as much of a sure thing as is possible in the oil business, but Gus says that he has everything he can handle right now. Gray tells Gus that he has no money. Gus says that he will have to let the option lapse and that the lease will go to Harry Nelson. Upon hearing this, Gray is galvanized into action. Nelson is the man who caused him to be unjustly court martialed in France. Gray came to Texas to get revenge upon Nelson. So Gray decides to market the lease. He uses his contact with the bankers to put together a deal in which Briskow makes $48,000. Briskow insists that he take half of it, and Gray is on his way to having the money he needs to undercut the financial dealings of Nelson. His method of revenge is not to be physical, but financial. He plans to break Nelson, who is a banker and oil investor in Wichita Falls.

Briskow wants Gray to take over the guidance of Buddy, but Gray says that he would be a bad model for him to follow and suggests instead that Gus hire a tutor for Buddy. Soon Buddy is sent off to school, and the rest of the family goes to a resort in some Eastern mountains. Mrs. Briskow loves the place because she goes up into the mountains and lives a fantasy life. Allie has her own tutor and studies hard and grows angry because she still sees herself crude and an object of humor to others. Her tutor keeps resigning, and Gus keeps raising her pay to keep her on. Gus spends most of his time at the livery stable in town.

Meanwhile, Gray has gone to Wichita Falls where he has met Mallow and a couple of con men and recruited them to work with him in breaking Harry Nelson. He goes to Nelson's office and tells him that he plans to break him but that he will do it honestly. Nelson feels threatened and starts to reach for a pistol he has in a drawer, but Gray warns him not to do that. They are finishing up their business when Miss. Good arrives. It turns out that she is Barbara Potter, daughter of the crusty old former sheriff, Tom Potter. Barbara has just returned from the East where she has been in school. Her father has spent all of his money on her education and has been scarcely working on his insurance business when she returns. So she has gone into oil scouting and has some business with Nelson. Nelson is interested in her romantically, but more interested in his oil business. Gray is smitten by her and starts courting her, sending her flowers and candy.

Gray gets the backing of several bankers in Dallas, and even as he is trying to hurt Nelson, he is making money in the oil business.

Gray decides to visit the Briskows at their hotel in the mountains. There things have been rocking along pretty well until the dancing teacher tries to kiss Allie. Allie socks him, and he insults her, telling her what a crude thing she is. She picks him up and throws him through the window. The manager of the hotel is about to throw the Briskows out when Gray arrives. He smooths things over, helps Mrs. Briskow dress, and participates in the fantasy life she leads in the mountains. He still thinks of Allie as a child though she is obviously in love with him.

Gray returns to his job of breaking Nelson financially. He learns that Barbara Parker has what she thinks is a great buy on a lease in the North Extension of Burkburnett. As he goes to look at the lease, we get a good picture of Burburnett: "Far away across the undulating prairie fields the horizon was broken by a low, dark barricade, the massed derricks of the town-site pool. So thickly were they grouped that they resembled a dense forest of high, black pines, and not until Gray drew closer could he note that this strange forest was leafless." (FG 215) The narrator tells about the long line of cars trying to get through Burburnett and being "carried along like chips in a stream of tar."(FG 215) He describes the sounds of the field: " . . . above the hum of idle motors could be heard the clank of pumps, the fitful coughing of gas engines, the hiss of steam. This, of course, was soon drowned in a terrific din of impatient horns, a blaring, brazen snarl at the delay. The whole line roared metallic curses at the cause of its stoppage." (FG 215)

Then through Gray's eyes, the narrator describes the Extension: Burkburnett had been laid out in lots and blocks, and the drilling had followed some sort of orderly system; but here were no streets, no visible plan. This had been a wheat field, and as well after well had come in, derricks, drilling rigs, buildings, tanks, piles of timber, and casing had been laid down with complete disregard of all save the owner's convenience." (FG 216) Cars had to drive around the maze of new pipes being laid.

He describes the new towns of canvas, board and corrugated iron which had sprung up. "By day they were mean, filthy, grotesque; by night they became incandescent, for every derrick was strung with lights, and the surplus supply of gas was burned in torches to prevent it from accumulating in ravines or hollows in explosive quantities. They were Mardi Gras cities." (FG 217)

When Gray arrives at the lease, Mr. Jackson, the owner of the lease, is not there. Gray waits, still no one. He goes into Newtown, and while he waits, he gambles. Some drunk keeps trying to take his chips. He grabs the drunk and throws him out of the place. Then Gray goes to eat. While he is eating, the same man comes in with a pistol. In trying to intimidate Gray, he hits a table and disturbs old Tom Parker. Parker threatens him, and he backs down, not appearing at all drunk. Parker has a "dog leg," a frontier Colt under his overcoat. Gray later learns from Tom Parker that the man who tried to kill him is a known killer, a man on the Nelson payroll.

Gray learns that the well he has been trying to buy is a phony. His con men cohorts have been trying to get Nelson to buy it, but he has passed on it because he is short of money. Gray's confederates explain to him:

"Well, then, it's salted!"

"Impossible! I saw it pumping."

"I'll say you did." Mallow chuckled. "Live oil, too; right out of old Mamma Earth. Cheap lease at seventy five thousand, eh? It's like this: the pipe line of the Atlantic runs across Jackson's lease, and one dark and stormy night he tapped it. It wasn't a hard thing to do; just took a little care and some digging. Now he runs the oil in, pumps it out and sells it back to them. He's a regular subsidiary of the great and only Atlantic Petroleum Company. It can't last long, of course, but—oh, what a well to hand Nelson! What a laugh it would have been!" (FG 226-7)

Gray tells them that he wants them to use only honest means to hurt Nelson. But they don't seem to pay much attention.

Word comes that Buddy has left school and is back in Dallas with a woman, Arline Montague. He loves her and plans to marry. Gray goes off to Dallas to see what he can do. He finds that Buddy is involved with an older woman, obviously a fortune hunter. Gray thinks he recognizes her but can't quite place her. He calls Mallow from Wichita Falls to help him. Mallow immediately recognizes her as Margie Fulton. He knew her from New Orleans where she was a "come on" for her husband's gambling house. Mallow tells Gray that Mrs. Fulton has a grown son. Mallow knows where he is, and Gray has him bring the son to Dallas to convince Buddy. Buddy won't listen to anything against his beloved, and Gray insists on trying to tell him, so they have a monstrous fist fight. Gray wins, but he is bruised and battered from the encounter. Mallow produces the boy, and Buddy is convinced. Gray feels bad about having ruined Mrs. Fulton's game, so he sets her and her son up in business in Wichita Falls running a café. Margie says, "Gee, Mr. Gray! I figured there must be some decent men in the world, but — I never thought I'd meet one." (FG 268) Buddy becomes a roughneck for Gray working near his old farm.

Meanwhile, Nelson can't seem to do anything right. He has to start drilling offsets to wells that Gray has completed. This gets expensive for him. He thinks he is buying a great lease in Arkansas, so he buys many acres. Then he discovers the water well and spring he trusted as signs of oil were salted. This time Gray's con men have succeeded, and they haven't even told Gray about the con. People find out about the con and are openly laughing at Henry Nelson, particularly the people he has sharped before.

Henry counterattacks by telling the local people about Gray's court-martial. Tom Parker is not happy about letting Gray pay court to his daughter if Gray has been in dereliction of duty. Gray says he will say no more to Barbara unless Tom agrees. Nelson also tries to get Gray's bankers to drop him by telling them about Gray's court-martial and his vendetta against Nelson. The banks are threatening to drop him, and Gray is hard pressed for cash. Gus Briskow offers to let Gray run all his business ventures, but Gray refuses.

Then his luck turns. Buddy calls to tell him that

he has a well that will produce two thousand barrels a day. How he could possibly know this since the well has not come in is not clear. Anyway, Gray goes to the well near the old farm. Allie has come at the same time, hoping to see Gray.

As Buddy is running the bailer, Gray stands by. Buddy is proud of what he has accomplished:

> Buddy Briskow was running the rig, and the dexterity with which he handled brake and control rod gave him pride. He had seated his sister on a bench out of the way, where she was protected from the drizzle, and he felt her eyes upon him. It gave him a sense of importance to have Allie watching him at such a crisis; he wished his parents were with her. If this well blew in big, as it seemed bound to do, it would be a personal triumph, for not many cub drillers could boast of bringing in a gusher the first time. It was, in fact, no mean accomplishment to make any sort of a well; to pierce the earth with an absolutely vertical shaft a half mile deep and line it with tons upon tons of heavy casing joined air-tight and fitted to a hair's breadth was an engineering feat in itself. It was something that only an oilman could appreciate. And he was an oil man; a darn good one, too, so Buddy told himself. (FG 305-6)

Shortly after this, the bailer sticks and Buddy sees a disaster about to occur: "Perhaps five hundred feet below, friction had checked its plunge, and meanwhile the velvet-running drum, spinning at its maximum velocity by reason of the whirling bull wheel, was unreeling its cable down upon the derrick platform. Down it poured in giant loops, and within those coils, either unconscious of his danger or paralyzed by its suddenness, stood Calvin Gray." (FG 306) Buddy slams into Calvin pushing him away. Then he is caught in the lines himself. He manages to free himself and go back to work:

> By this time the whole structure of the derrick was rocking to the mad gyrations of the bull wheel; the giant spool was spinning with a speed that threatened to send it flying, like the fragments of a bursting bomb, but the youth understood dimly the danger of stopping it too suddenly—to fetch up that plunging weight at the cable end might snap the line, collapse the derrick, "jim" the well. Buddy weaved dizzily in his tracks, nevertheless, his hand was steady, and he applied a gradually increasing pressure to the brake. Nor did he take his eyes from his task until the drum had ceased revolving and the runaway bailer hung motionless in the well. (FG 215)

But Gray is seriously injured by the push and fall and has to be carried back to the Briskow farm. There Allie nurses him.

The well turns out be a gasser. Buddy says that the gas will be worth as much as the oil would have. Then Allie sees the night turn into day. The well is on fire. Miraculously, the well puts itself out. When the derrick burns, "the stack of drill stem fell in such a way as to close the gate valve at the top of the casing." (FG 314)

While Buddy is working at the well, a storm comes, and the Briskow farm is flooded and cut off from every road out. The water keeps rising, and then lightning starts hitting wells around the farm. Five wells are burning finally, and there is oil in the water. Allie and Gray fear for their lives. Allie wants Gray to love her, but he continues to treat her as a child. She is angry and heartbroken about his attitude. Finally the rain lets up, and Buddy is able to get to them. Gray takes them into his confidence about his dealings with Nelson, asking for their help. They agree to help him. He will also talk to Gus about backing him. He tells Buddy about work and the power of money:

> You took hold of this field work and ran it like a man. I said you'd make a hand, and you have. The day is coming when people like you, who went from poverty to affluence overnight, will retrace that journey. That's the time when the truly dramatic story of the Texas oil boom will be written. Then will come the real tragedy, and you mustn't be caught in it. Money isn't a servant, Buddy; it is a master, and a mighty stern, relentless master, at that. When your first well blew in, it didn't mean ease and enjoyment, as you thought; it meant hard work for the rest of your life. (FG 215)

Buddy tells Gray that he is almost sure that the fire at their well was started by one of Nelson's men. Gray takes Buddy to Wichita Falls with him so that he can begin to learn the financial part of the business. He introduces him to Barbara Parker, and Buddy instantly falls in love with her. Unaware of this, Gray has Buddy go out into the field with her to learn about leasing.

Soon the moment of confrontation comes with Henry Nelson and his father. At the meeting of the board of directors of the bank, the Nelsons learn that the Briskows have bought the controlling interest. Gray finally explains how Nelson had set him up and how he had been convicted on trumped-up charges. And he tells the other directors, who are local ranchers, that Henry had also been convicted in a court martial.

After taking control of the bank, the Briskows and Gray learn that the Nelson's have used bank funds to cover their oil losses. Finally, Gray has Henry where he wants him. Henry blames his father, but Gray will not let him off the hook. Henry is forced to sign a confession about all of his chicanery in France. Gray stops his campaign against him but does plan to turn him over to the authorities for his stealing from the bank.

Then he plans to start romancing Barbara Potter, but before he can do that, Tom Parker tells him that Barbara is engaged to Buddy. Heartbroken and depressed, Gray leaves town immediately. He stops in Dallas to visit Mrs. Briskow, who has been sick. There he is mothered by her and then Allie. It is now obvious that in time Allie will have Gray for her own. So all is neatly settled in the end.

In the next oil novel of North Central Texas, banks also play a critical role, this time a possible bank failure. It is *Out of the Ground* (1937) by Norma Patterson, a professional novelist, and Crate Dalton, her husband and a lawyer. The protagonist, David Nelson, is also a lawyer, a young one, returning to Waldo, the town he lived in as a child. It is a fictional boomtown near Ranger. Nelson arrives one day, and an old rancher and former friend of his father's, Solomon White, figures a way for him to have an office in the overcrowded town. White hauls his smoke house to town and sets it up, even providing David some leftover wallpaper. The first day there he gets a case. An old rancher, Mr. Dyer, is being sued by his neighbor, Mr. Lewis, an oil man, about a dog. The oil man had picked up the Dyer's dog in the field and given it to his son, Tim. When Mr. Dyer's daughter, Christine, found out where the dog was, she went to get it. Lewis sued. David represents Dyer in the case and wins, but in doing so he ridicules and makes an enemy of Red Teer, Lewis's driller. David has taken a liking to Nan Whitely, a local reporter, and discovers only after the case that Teer is her fiancé. Soon Lewis is killed in an oil-well accident, and Tim is taken in by the Dyers. Because Tim has inherited everything from his father and there is no other family, Red Teer wants to be Tim's guardian. Nan persuades him that his doing so would not be the best for the child.

David increases his law practice and becomes a member of the board of directors of a new bank. It starts making money immediately. The price of oil is $3.50, and new wells and fields are being opened up. David has avoided speculating in oil, but one day Tom Ezell, a local farmer, comes to him with a proposal. Tom wants David to make a lease agreement for him. For this Tom wants him to take one third of all the revenue. David tries to persuade

Tom that that is too much, but after Tom insists, David agrees.

David decides to see Red Teer's well come in. It is a gusher and almost immediately catches fire. Several men are killed, and Red is knocked to the ground unconscious. Nan rushes forward to try to get him away from the fire. David gets there and with difficulty pulls him away. Nan is appreciative of David's help, but she still plans to marry Teer. David makes arrangement for and supervises putting the well fire out. Once again we get a clear picture of how wells are extinguished.

David meets Mr. Warren, head of Western Oil, and David is quite taken with Warren's beautiful daughter, Eva. Warren has an agreement with several of David's clients to drill a well on their property. The agreement reads that if no oil is reached by the depth of 3,500 feet, Western oil will retain rights to the leases.

The Ezell well comes in a gusher, and David is suddenly quite wealthy. Tom Ezell makes one last trip on his nitroglycerin truck, and he is blown to bits. David is left with the responsibility of seeing after Tom's wife, Min.

David and Eva Warren become romantically involved. The reader is more aware than David about the shallow, selfishness of Eva. But soon David is in conflict with her father over the lease deal. Warren is trying to cheat his clients by saying that they have reached 3,500 feet and that Western should receive the leases. David finds out from Nan that the well has only reached 3,200 feet. It's a scheme by Western to get the leases without having to pay for them. Warren confronts David and demands the leases. David refuses him, and Bullard, Western's strong-arm man, tries to take the leases by force. David pulls a pistol on him, so Warren and Bullard leave angry. David wins out eventually, and Western goes back to drilling and brings in a producing well. The quarrel between Warren and David is patched up by Eva, and they become engaged.

But oil prices plummet. Soon David and all of Waldo reach a financial crisis. The bank is in danger of failing. The Dyers and David agree to put up their own money to keep the bank from defaulting. The crowd trying to attack the bank is being led by Bullard, Warren's man, who now hates David. David and the Dyers keep the mob in check. Even Tim and Bozo, the dog, come to their aid. Finally Nan brings the Texas Rangers to their rescue. David has to go to Ft. Worth to get the money from the bank in order to pay off the creditors. He goes by to see Eva, who tells him that she will not marry him if he gives his money to pay the creditors. He feels honor bound to do so. So their relationship ends.

David has to have the money, $350,000, to the Waldo bank by a certain time, and he has trouble getting it there because of a terrible thunderstorm that he has to drive through. Finally he arrives, and the bank is saved, but only after all of the bad debts are removed. The Dyers and David will have to collect money on these debts in order to get any of their money back. They discover that Red Teer has taken his money out of the bank and left owing them for the cabletool rigs. When Nan discovers this, she is through with Teer.

David discovers that Western Oil is trying to move their mortgaged equipment out of the field, and he and the marshal go there to prevent it. Bullard tries to push through, but the marshal shoots the tires out on his trucks. Bullard charges David, and they fight. During the scuffle, they fall off a ledge. David hits Bullard one last time, and Bullard is knocked out. David passes out and is taken to the hospital. Nan brings flowers, and they agree to team up — romantically and professionally. They each have a little money left, and they will begin again, but the oil boom is over in Waldo. They will move to Mexia.

Chapter 12

Rich Kid Toughens Up

Like Buddy, Jim McNeely, Kimball Wingate, and others, the young protagonist of J. C. Rickman's *Racing Bits* (1926) is transformed by his work in the oilfield. In 1920 as the novel begins, Chuck Carruthers approaches his old friend from the Alaska Gold Rush days, John Burkitt, and asks him for a loan of $100,000 in order to drill a wildcat well. The chances of it being successful in the area just north of Breckenridge are higher than normal, but it must be drilled in a very short time and must be a producer or the lease will revert to the seller, one Sled Jones. Jones, an unscrupulous individual, wants to get the lease back because he already has another buyer lined up, a Mr. Napier.

Although Burkitt, an extremely rich Chicago financier, knows that he might lose the $100,000 if the well is a duster, he eagerly agrees to make the loan because of the trust he puts in his old friend. Carruthers says that he wants to make the well successful because he wants the money for his beloved daughter, Ione. Burkitt confides in Carruthers about the difficulties he is having with his son, John Burkitt, Jr. John Jr. is already an alcoholic at twenty. He gets women in trouble and wastes money — is just generally irresponsible. To get him out of his latest scrape, Carruthers agrees to take him to the oilfield to try to make a man out of him.

On first arriving in Breckenridge, John is conned out of his only cash in a stock scam. Carruthers tells him that his father has suspended his allowance and that he will have to make it on his own in the field. So John goes to work, beginning with the tiring and difficult task of carrying the heavy timbers used to build a derrick. He is in great pain, but he manages to stick, getting a little stronger after the first week. Soon he is working with the scarred veteran driller, Tom Jeffries. Things begin to go well with John but less well for the drilling operation because Sled Jones and Napier are trying to sabotage the drilling. Napier, who is drilling a well nearby, sends a man in the night to destroy the dam. John fights with him and gets the worst of it, but he is able to drive him away.

John hasn't even wanted a drink since he has been working on the rig, but he is persuaded by one of the other tool dressers to go into one of the many joints in Breckenridge. There he overhears the other tool dresser making an agreement to sabotage the well. He breaks into the conversation. And once again he loses the fight, but he scares off the tool dresser and Mr. Napier. So he has saved the operation again.

John has meanwhile met and fallen in love with Ione Carruthers. He agrees to drive her from the well to Graham where she is staying with friends. They are caught in a terrible storm. He drives through water and mud and finally gets her safely to Graham. He wants to rush straight back to the well because he knows he is needed, but he falls asleep and sleeps two days. After returning to the well, he gets a nice note from Ione, but he is shy about expressing his affection for her.

As the deadline draws near, there is still another attempt to destroy the well. Once again, John is instrumental in foiling the attackers. Then tragedy strikes. Carruthers is severely injured in an accident involving ropes and the bullwheel. John drives him to Graham. He is near death, but John leaves him in order to return to the well. In the absence of Carruthers, as son of the leading investor in the well, John takes control and pushes the operation forward. They need another driller, so he advertises his need. Sled Jones and Napier show up and say that Napier is a driller. John becomes so incensed that he attacks them with his fists. This time he wins. They are thrown out even though Jones owns the property. And they don't return. Carruthers dies, and Burkitt, Sr., arrives. He grieves for his friend but is greatly pleased with what a man Carruthers has made out of his errant son.

The well comes in just in time and is a major producer. Ione sells the lease for a huge sum to a large oil company. John and she become engaged, and John plans to go into the oil business with his old mentor, Tom Jeffries. So we have another generic oilfield novel with a young man being toughened up and improved by the hard work on an oil rig and by the sage advice of an older oil driller.

Chapter 13

The Senator's Son

Another North Central Texas oilfield novel, *Fort Worth* (1984) by Leonard Sanders[1], is a saga of the Spurlock family. Clay Spurlock is the son of Senator Travis Spurlock, and in the third section of the novel starting in 1915, "the Boom Years," Clay — young, impetuous, daring — goes out on his own to make a fortune. He chooses the oilfield though he has no knowledge of oil or the oil business. He visits the oilfield and talks to the drillers to learn what he can. He talks to one driller, Pete Pierson, for several hours. Finally, Pierson decides Clay needs to see the well. Clay spends several days there learning first hand, gaining information he could never have learned from a book.

Clay likes Pierson, so he gets him to join him in a partnership. They find a spot to drill in "rugged mesquite-infested country north of Wichita Falls." (*FW* 236) It is owned by an old rancher who is "lean and weathered as a bois d'arc fence post." (*FW* 236) They convince him to lease to them,and Clay uses up all his available cash in doing so. Clay approaches his older brother, Durwood, a banker, about making a loan. Durwood says, "The bank can't gamble with its money and that's all this is. A gamble, pure and

---

[1] Sanders (1929-2005) worked on newspapers in Wichita Falls, Enid, Okla., Oklahoma City, and Fort Worth and is the author of several novels.

simple." (FW 239) Clay leaves angrily. He starts drilling and is sure the well is going to be a good producer, but he is about to have his rig seized. He talks the supplier into two additional days to raise the money to pay him.

Then Clay works on "front." He drives to Fort Worth, goes to the finest male emporium, and orders two dark conservative suits of the best quality. Then he says, "Shoes of English leather. A homburg. Spats. The whole works." He adds a gold-headed cane, and he is ready to go see the Wichita Falls banker. He lays out in detail what he needs and what he will do for the bank. The banker notices his clothes:

> The banker's gaze flicked to the cut of Clay's suit, the cravat, the gold-headed cane. He sighed. "I see your point, Mr. Spurlock. You understand, of course, that your request is highly unorthodox. Ordinarily, we wouldn't even consider such a thing. But we've learned in the last few months that the oil business is like no other. Incidentally, I once met your father, and have always held him in highest regard. I'm glad you've chosen our bank. I think we can do business. (FW 245)"

He gets the banker not to file the mortgage lien right away so that he can go into the field and lease the property adjoining his well. Clay wants to sell the whole operation to Majestic oil and go look for another place to drill. Pierson wants to stay and drill other wells. Finally, they toss a coin and Clay wins. Clay and Pete sell the well and leases for $150,000.

Soon afterwards, they sink a dry hole in Oklahoma near Cushing and lose much of what they made. They start on a new well, running a poor-boy operation. They start getting caving. So they need to run casing, but if they buy casing, they won't have money to drill. Then Pete tells Clay how to steal casing by "jarring": "You simply lower a bundle of dynamite down the pipe, with wires attached. You put a collar on the top of the casing and put it under a good strain with a hydraulic jack. Then you hook your detonator to the coil on your truck. The blast blows the casing apart. If you're lucky, the upper part of the pipe is jarred loose. You can pull it up with a block and sheave." (FW 277) Pete tells him about some wells near Strawn, so Clay starts jarring. After a few successful jobs, he has to blow one casing twice. Then a rifle-toting ranch wife shows up. She is not fooled by his fast talking, but she does show an attraction to him. Their flirtation will lead to a long-term sexual relationship.

The well comes in as a barely profitable producer. Pete Pierson skids the rig and start proving up the field, and Clay looks for other prospective places to drill. He leases some land near Hog Creek, later called Desdemona, just because he has the feel that there is oil there.

Shortly after this, Clay meets Leigh Ann. She had been engaged to Clay's brother, Vern, who was killed flying in France. She has married Lester Wilson, but Lester is a real loser. Clay gets in a fight with him, flattens him, and takes Leigh Ann away. This of course causes quite a flap in Ft. Worth society. Lester files charges against him. Clay buys him off, and a divorce is granted in September. In October, their first son, Broderick is born.

Soon the Ranger oilfield blows in huge, and Clay is there to take advantage of it. He gets some of the very best leases, and they hit it big. They are so busy that they hardly have a rig available to drill in Hog Town where he had leased the land earlier. Soon, Pete and Clay are exceedingly rich. Clay becomes a legend in the oilfield:

> He seemed to possess the uncanny knowledge of exactly when and where he was needed. He usually arrived unannounced at some remote drill site, eyes red-rimmed from lack of sleep and many miles of hard driving, a woman asleep in the front seat of his car. After checking the core tests and logs, he would guide the well through the final phase of drilling, when fast judgments were crucial. On completion of the well he would give a new set of instructions to the driller and drive away. Sometimes, when the drill bit had not yet reached the pay zone, he would park behind the toolshed and party all night with the woman, emerging every hour or so, half drunk, to check the progress of the drill stem and to complain to the driller, "Hell, I'm making hole faster than that."
>
> The stories become legion. It is said he once brought in an eight-hundred barrel well in Burkburnett one afternoon, drove to Breckenridge and danced for hours, whipped two men in a fistfight at three in the morning, and left for Desdemona, where he brought in a two-thousand barrel gush-

er a few hours after dawn. (*FW* 338)

But he is completely disorganized, and Pete is not happy about it:

> "Clay, God damn it, this whole thing is getting out of hand. You've made deals all over West Texas without a word in writing. We have wells in production with royalty split sixty ways from Sunday, and some of the checks are months in arrears. You've probably got millions of dollars worth of paper riding around in the bottom of your toolbox. We have six accountants in five towns working on our books, and not one of them has the slightest suspicion that the others exist. I haven't any idea what our bank balances are, and I'll bet you don't either. We've got drillers, landsmen, and God knows who out there writing checks on us, with no control whatsoever. It's got to stop!" (*FW* 339)

So Spurlock oil builds a large showy office building in Ft. Worth, and Pete does what he can to keep the books straight.

In 1918, Clay's father, Senator Travis Spurlock, dies. Somehow Durwood has managed to get himself named as beneficiary of everything, and there is a big squabble over the house. Travis doesn't care, but he vows to get even with Durwood for his sister. He has two more children, Loren and Crystelle. And he builds a large house for them and for his sister. Things are going well until Pete is killed when the derrick is pulled down onto him, much like an accident in California in Robert Hyde's *Crude*. Clay mourns for his friend, then settles financially with Pete's wife Betty, and he is the sole owner of Spurlock oil.

To get revenge on his brother, Clay sees to it that Durwood has the opportunity to buy some worthless oil stock. When the crash comes in 1929, Durwood discovers his stock is worthless and that he cannot pay the bank back for money he took from it to buy the stock. So he shoots himself. Clay has lots of oil in the ground and owes nothing, so he just sits back and waits out the slump. But he meets his end in an oil well accident. He is drilling his deepest hole ever, 11,000 feet deep, when he runs into trouble. Koon, his dependable driller, sees it happening:

> The heavy drilling mud was boiling up in the casing. Bubbles of gas popped to the surface. Koon watched in disbelief. The column of heavy mud two miles high was exerting unimagined weight on the bottom of the hole.
>
> But something down there was fighting back with even greater strength. The derrick began to tremble.
>
> Koon put his hand to the casing. He could feel vibrations traveling up through more than eleven thousand feet of pipe.
>
> "Get off this fucking rig!" he yelled. "She's going to blow!"
>
> The roughnecks ran to the edge of the floor and jumped. A rumble came from deep within the earth. Koon glanced up. The derrickman was sliding down his safety line.
>
> The drilling mud gurgled and spat a solid

stream several feet into the air. Another rumble came from the earth. The derrick floor shook.

Koon needed no further warning. He ran to the edge of the floor and; jumped. He landed with a painful jolt and fell sprawling. Behind him he heard the torturous scrape of ripping metal. Gas roared out of the hole, spewing mud and sand into the dangling draw works. (FW 397-8)

Clay comes running out of the driller's shack, sees all this, and asks Koon if he turned on the blowout preventer. Koon says there wasn't time, and Clay starts for the well. Koon tries to stop him, but Clay hits him and goes to his death:

Clay was turning the metal valve wheel when the thunderous rumbling in the earth resumed, increasing, traveling upward. Lying flat more than fifty yards away, Koon was jolted into the air. He had a glimpse of a scene that was seared into his brain forever. Struggling with the valve wheel, Clay suddenly was enveloped in an exploding sheet of flame. The derrick, draw works, ninety-foot stands of pipe, all the ponderous machinery were sent hurtling skyward. Twisted steel and drill pipe fell like metal hail.

The roaring column of gas snorted and screamed as it hurled mud, sand, and rocks out of the crater where the derrick had stood. With another convulsive roar, hundreds of feet of casing soared into the air followed by a pillar of fire. (FW 398-9)

After Clay's death, his oldest son, Brod, who is

still in college studying geology, has to take over the business or sell out. He decides he will take over. He does this with some difficulty because the business of running the company has been neglected in favor of seeking even more oil. Clay had most of the company records in his head. No one knows much about anything. Brod has to assert his authority and take charge of the business until his brother, Loren, graduates from business college. Managing the company would be hard enough under the best of circumstances, but like H. L. Hunt, Clay has two other families, with grown children, one of whom, Grover, has spent lots of time in the field with his father and is interested in becoming a part of the business. The complications are worked out, and Brod, Loren, and Grover manage Spurlock Oil successfully. In the end, there are interfamily difficulties leading to conflict and death. But little of the last third of the book has to do with the discovery or production of oil.

Ft. Worth has much in it about the discovery, financing, and production of oil, but it is much more. It is both a family and city history. It is a big book, filled with many historical characters, ones such as novelist Katherine Anne Porter, wolf-catcher Jack Abernathy, dancers Vernon and Irene Castle, and evangelist J. Frank Norris. It's an interesting, well-written novel, and the oil part seems to be particularly well done.

Chapter 14

Harvard Man

The most recent of the oilfield novels of North Central Texas is supposedly set in Abilene. If so, it's a much smaller, more podunky Abilene. *Chocolate Lizards* (1999) by Cole Thompson is an odd novel – it's an out-and-out unmitigated farce. It, is told by a rather straitlaced individual. The narrator, Erwin Vandermeer, describes the eccentricities of his business associate, Merle Luskey. Luskey, a drilling contractor, hires Erwin, an out-of-work actor and Harvard graduate, as a roughneck on one of his rigs. Then he uses him to do many genuinely difficult things, simply because he is a college man. In spite of Abilene's three universities, no one in this Abilene seems to be educated.

Merle is colorful. And he's crude, drunken, bizarre. He tells Erwin about himself and his dreams:

> He leans over, lays his hand on my shoulder, and squeezes. "I like you, son. Now my boy, God bless his ass, I love him, but he ain't worth a shit. Butchoo now, you done gone to college and ever'thayng, nd by God, you just listen to me cuz I'm gonna tell ya somethin'." He squeezes my shoulder harder. "I may not be the smartest sumbitch 'at ever pulled on a pair uh boots, but I know a thayng or two about drillin' a hole, and I

know a thayng or two about fightin' fer a dream. I come up from a short-pay roughneck all the way to ownin' six uh my own rigs. Six, boy. Five National doubles and a Connie-Em triple. 'At's what I always wanted, ownin' my own rigs, and by God I got 'em." He takes an ice-clinking sip of Jack Daniel's. "Now you listen here. If it's in yer blood to be in the movies—and ain't nobody can answer 'at butchoo—then you got a problem, boy. If ya ever wanna be happy in this life, if ya ever wanna be worth yer boots and be able to look yerself in the mirror and say, 'Kiss my ass,' then yer gonna have to fight, son. Yer gonna have to fight like a goddam Mexican bull. Cuz I tell ya, dreams don't come easy. I don't care what it is—bein' in the movies, ownin' a drillin' outfit, or bein' governor uh Texas—dreams don't come easy. Yer gonna get kicked in the head and shot in the ass a hunerd times, butcha gotta just stand right back up, swalluh yer teeth, and keep swangin'. Cuz 'ere ain't no other options, see? If ya just give up and try to ignore it and go on, you'll be the sourest sumbitch 'at ever rolled out uh bed and pulled on a pair uh boots." (CL 51-2)

Erwin goes to work roughnecking, and there is lots of good information about the drilling techniques employed on the rigs. Then the plot gets weird. The local bank is in cahoots with the sheriff to repossess all of Merle's drilling rigs. In fact, the bank has already resold them even though he still has time to pay his note. Merle sees his only way out is to find a lease and drill his own well. Merle and Erwin spy on a large oil company using concealed cameras to get seismographic information. With this, they find out that there is one prime drilling site available in another county north of Abilene. It's on land owned by an eccentric rancher, Alton Scheermeyer, who has threatened to shoot any oil man who comes on his property. Merle and Erwin go onto Alton's land, lying to him, saying they are cattlemen. They discover that Alton's main entertainment is reading Penthouse magazine. So Merle goes to Dallas to get a woman to come out to the ranch and persuade Alton to lease. It works, but Merle falls for her himself. They get the lease, but before they can start drilling, they have to avoid arrest by imprisoning the sheriff and his deputies and taking them to the drilling site before releasing them. The sheriff vows to get revenge

To get the well drilled quickly, Merle becomes super-driller, working tirelessly night and day. One of the strangest scene in any oil novel occurs when Sheriff Nall attacks the drilling rig, using Sheriff's department helicopters. Nall's men shoot at all of the boiler's trying to sabotage the job. Merle is hit in the chest, but he discovers that the bullet struck his whiskey flask, so he is soaked but unhurt. Then Nall's men start shooting the fuel tanks by the rigs. Alton, the old rancher, shows up with a goose gun and hits the helicopter, and it goes off trailing black smoke. Within nine hours, the crew has made repairs and are drilling again.

Soon through the heroic efforts of Merle, the string is ready to reach pay, and one of the roughnecks, Virgil, asks him if he is going to test. He says he is: "He hoists up the almost nine-thousand-feet-long drill string. The kelly rises into the derrick and the top joint of drill pipe rises through the rotary table about four feet. Mud oozes down its side and spills onto the floor." (CL 236) He tells them to "hang her up in the slips." (CL 236) He then has them kill the engine and break the connection between the kelly and the last joint of pipe. Virgil is worried, "Shit, boss, we ain't hardly got any mud in the hole. We just cut a helluva show. What if she blows out?" (CL 236) About this time the helicopters come back, accompanied by police cars and swat troops. So Virgil and Erwin break the connection. And the top joint is left to stand open a few feet above the rotary table. It starts to gurgle water, and Merle asks for and installs an orbit valve. The fountain of water gets stronger, shooting several feet up. Merle stands beside it and swigs from his bottle of Jack Daniels. He talks to the well. "Atta baby! C'mon and blow for Daddy!" (CL 237) Then he tells Mule and Shay, two crewmembers, to get back. Shay says, "What if you cain't shut her in." (CL 237) Merle swigs again and says, "Bullshit, I'll shut her in. Get back." (CL 237) They leave and the water continues to flow. The cops arrive. Merle pours a little of his Jack Daniels into the water coming from the well and says, "Here, darling, have a taste." (CL 237) Then he says, "Now, c'mon. They're bout to take ever' Goddamn thayng I ever worked for." (CL 237) Then, startled by the helicopters, Alton's cattle stampede.

The banker arrives with authorizations signed by the local county officials, and he tells Sheriff Nall to go up to Merle on the rig and serve them. There is thunder suddenly. At first they think that it is the cattle again. But no, it's the well. Everything immediately becomes drenched in a shower of oil. The banker and sheriff, soaked already, run for their car. Merle shuts off the flow. With oil dripping from his hard hat, he stumbles toward his crew, swigging from his bottle. Then he goes up to the banker's car. Don starts to leave, and Merle hollers after him, "Hey, wait, Don't run off. I want to buy yer Goddam bank, Don! Hey!" (CL 244)

So Merle pays off his note. Erwin gets his pay, and a $500 bonus and heads back to Hollywood. He doesn't know what his future holds. But he is going to keep on fighting and be worth his boots, the chocolate lizards of the title, boots given to him by Merle. The basic plot is so far-fetched, and Merle's character so extreme, it's difficult to take the novel seriously. Fortunately, we don't have to. There's lots of good oil stuff here. There are almost essay-like explanations on how a rotary rig works. The dust jacket says that Cole Thompson, the author, has worked in an oilfield.

The oil novels of North Central Texas are more about banking than those of other areas probably because of the coming of the great depression so shortly after many of the fields were developed. Another possible cause was the excess production of oil and its consequently lower price. These novels are also, like those set in other areas, about the generic oilfield hero, from Buddy to Erwin, young men being toughened up through working in the oilfield.

Oil Novels
of
East
Texas

Chapter 15

Drilling in the Piney Woods

Blacks had been denied an active role in the oilfield from its earliest times. They were only allowed to hold the most menial of positions. In novels about the early oilfields, there is hardly even a mention of them. In *Black Gold* by Jewel Gibson, blacks work feeding and caring for stock, but are not allowed to work as mule skinners. In *Fever in the Earth*, blacks do drive oxen teams in Beaumont, but when going into Sour Lake on the edge of the big thicket, they are warned to be away before nightfall. They are described as digging ditches for a pipeline crew, but in Sour Lake, their camp is attacked by a group of whites, and they are driven out even though the contractor has not been able to hire whites for the hard, dirty low-paying work. More blacks live and own land in Northeast Texas, and they figure prominently in the oil novels of the area.

In the first work of fiction about the East Texas oilfield, a black farm family falls victim to the oil boom. This first work was not a novel but a short story by Winifred Sanford, "Fever in the South," first published in November 1931 in The *American Mercury*, only one year after the famous Daisy Bradford #3 was brought in by Dad Joiner on September 5, 1930. Sanford's husband was an oil lawyer working out of Longview, and Sanford had an opportunity to see the boom first hand. (W iv) Her story is written in four parts. The first is from the point of view of Mr. Donavan, an experienced wildcatter. Although determined to quit wildcatting, he is on his way to the new East Texas oilfield. We see it first from his viewpoint:

> Ahead of him, as far off as he could see, were other trucks with their trailers, and other cars slithering along in the soft red mud. Drilling rigs, which had been lying idle for a couple of years, likely in West Texas and Oklahoma and New Mexico, were moving in. He saw slush pumps and boilers and drill pipe and casing. And everything else that went with a boom — oilfield workers in old Fords; promoters, like himself, in Buicks or Cadillacs; hamburger stands on wheels; wagons loaded with household goods; and all the way along, rain or no rain, the hitchhikers, with their coat collars turned up, and their paper bundles under their arms, begging for rides. (W 148)

Donavan says that he is broke and that he won't drill again, maybe he will trade some leases. He already has more oil than he can sell. But he gets caught up in the excitement with people talking about fifty-thousand barrel wells. He just needs to know where to drill. He needs a "first-class fortune-teller" like Rita, who advised him in Borger.

The next section is from Rita's viewpoint. She has just arrived with her husband, Tom, who serves meals. They wake up wet from their camping. They slept in their clothes the first night on a mattress and springs on the ground. She goes looking for water, carrying two buckets. She reports on what she sees:

> Well, here she was at the crossroads. There were a few buildings which must have been here before the boom, a drugstore and a cafe and a general store and a church—but all around, everywhere, were new pine shacks and corrugated iron warehouses. And cars! The cars were packed in so solid you could have stepped from one to the other clear down to the tracks without ever setting your foot on the ground. And sitting on the running boards and bumpers were the bums, all kinds of them, old fellows with whiskers and no teeth, the boys with thin white hands, and now and then an honest to-God oilfield worker out of a job. (*W* 150)

Rita enjoys the new field with all of its excitement. She gets back to the campsite and her husband tells her Donovan is there wanting advice. She puts on her scarf and thinks that telling him where to drill ought to be easy considering all the oil in East Texas.

The third section is from the viewpoint of a black family suddenly invaded by Donovan, who wants to lease their land. They don't have any idea what he is talking about, but they are afraid of him and all White men. When Donavan drives away, the husband confused asks, "What he mean?" His wife says, "I dunno. But he don't mean no good, that's sure. He don't mean no good." (*W* 158)

In the fourth section, we see the boom from old Miss Carrie's point of view. She runs Mr. Donavan's boarding house, and he is taking her to see his well. She gives an accounting of the changes in her town:

> Besides, this trip to the well was Mr. Donovan's idea and not hers — even though she was curious to see this oil which had already made such a difference in her daily life. Who would have supposed, two months ago, that she would rent out her guest room, with its old walnut furniture, or the other room, which had been her son's before he married? Or that Savannah would leave her, after sixteen years, to work in the hotel? Or that the town, where she had lived all her life in peace and quiet, would be so crowded with strangers that she would have to force her way through its streets? Or that the corridor of the red brick courthouse would be blocked with tables and chairs and girls copying records on typewriters? Or that the church where she had worshipped for fifty years would be sold to make room for an office building? (W 159)

Miss Carrue is also disconcerted by the strange habits of her boarders. She continues thinking about all the changes that have taken place, about all the new people, the beggars and the peddlers. She had been used to poverty, but this was different, "something a great deal lower than poverty" (W 161)

Mr. Donavan tells her that he got lucky. He followed the advice of a fortune teller, and he hit oil eighteen miles from the nearest well. He also tells her that some sharper had talked the black family into selling their royalty for five hundred dollars just a few days before he struck oil. She sees the black couple moving out and wonders where they will go. As the story ends she is becoming despondent:

> She was very tired, and the smell of gas and oil had made her a little sick. Resting her head in the corner, she closed her eyes and clasped her gloves in her lap. It would have been better, she told herself, if she had stayed at home this morning. The well had been so little to see; and the old Negro moving out — that troubled her. It made her wonder if sooner or later, they would not all of them be turned out of their homes — if they were not all of them, like Esau of old, selling their birthright for a mess of pottage. (W 163)

This story presents a remarkably succinct and vivid picture of the new East Texas oilfield by a writer who knew the area first hand.

Chapter 17

Family Style

Karle Wilson Baker, a native of East Texas, also uses her experience there to draw a vividly realistic picture. The first novel about East Texas oil is her *Family Style* (1937). Baker lived just south of the great oil pool, in Nacogdoches, where she taught creative writing at Stephen F. Austin State College.

The title of her novel, *Family Style*, is a double entendre, reflecting the way members of one family reacted to the coming of oil and the way food was often served at oilfield restaurants.

There was an East Texas style to an oil boom, too. Here the people holding the land were mostly poor farmers, black and White. Here the derricks were made out of green pine and erected in the midst of the same pines. Here there is lots of rain, lots of red mud.

This is one of the few oil novels with a female protagonist, Kathleen Priest. As the novel begins, Kathleen is still in love with and married to Duke Priest although Duke has been having an affair with a fellow employee of the Ford agency in the small town of Sardis. Duke knows she knows, but Kathleen has said nothing. Oil has been discovered near the Priest farm. And a derrick has been erected on it by a small-time oil producer, Mr. Trumpler. The first scenes are at the newly erected derrick where

Kathleen is considering how the coming of oil will affect her family. Duke's father, Matthew Priest, has farmed with only moderate success, raising his children just above poverty. His daughter, Ella, has one year of college and has returned home and seems to be destined to be an old maid. The youngest son, Dave, is a teenager. The oldest son has his own farm nearby and is also just getting by. Matthew's wife is a straitlaced religious type and fears the wealth that the well may bring. Her daughter agrees with her. Matthew is eager to have the well and the money it will bring as are Duke and Kathleen. There are also two other important Priests, the cousins Fred and Harlowe. Fred is the over-aggressive, ambitious family member, the closest thing we have to a villain in the novel. Harlowe is easy going but inappropriately married to a beautiful, dissatisfied woman, Rose Anne.

As Kathleen sits at the derrick thinking, she is joined by the orphan, Henry, who is the ward of Uncle Fin. Henry is one of her students at the local school, and he loves her and Duke only. Most people seem to just barely tolerate him, thinking him a warty homeless waif. She likes Henry and likes to visit with him in this leisurely way when she can. She grew up almost an orphan herself. Her mother died when she was quite young, and her father, Dr. Kerry, never quite got over it, becoming somewhat of a recluse, one who drank much too much. Her grandfather had been a highly successful doctor and had a large estate with a mansion. Before the younger Dr. Kerry died, he had run through the estate, and upon his death, there was only a family burial plot left. He had willed a house to the former family servant, Sally. This old black woman and Kathleen still love each other. About all that remains of the family's former prominence is that the name of the community in which Sally lives is Kerryville.

In order to break from his romantic relationship and to get into the oilfield action, Duke takes a job in Tyler, replacing a trucking owner, Mr. Bramlett, who had been killed in an accident. This is the only oil novel that treats in detail the difficulties of trucking the equipment into the oilfield. It tells about Duke's actions and reactions to his new job:

> There were five giant trucks (besides the "crip") which Bramlett had been keeping busy day and night; Duke's first job was to get them all back into action. It would have been a simple enough undertaking, with his experience of such work, if oilfields in the boom-stage were served by highways, or even by ordinary country roads. A part of Duke's everyday work was the scouting of road-conditions, finding new travel-lanes as new locations were made in the dips among the pine hills, working out a new way around a quagmire which had become impassable. He liked the work, in spite of the long hours and the pitiless labor that it imposed: liked the struggle with earth and weather, liked being a part of the excitement and suspense and frenzied activity. His will was pitted against all sorts of obstacles, and his pride constantly at stake, in the-game of keeping his five grunting monsters always at work. No matter how many others broke down, no matter

how many wheels churned helplessly in the black mud or spun in the hub-deep sand, his must keep moving.

He liked the men who worked for him. Some were mere boys from the surrounding farms, much like the boy he had been a few years before; others were case-hardened specimens of a sort with which he had never before come to close quarters. He found himself developing, almost irrespective of their other qualities, a sort of doting pride in their hardihood, their rough resourcefulness and skill, in each man's tightjawed determination to get his own load to its predestined place, whether it were possible or not. "More than half the job is the driver," he would hear himself expounding to his small employer, whose somber, appraising eyes never left his face as he talked. "You've got to trust 'em, to a certain extent; let 'em know you count on 'em. Sooner or later, the best equipment will bog down or turn over, unless you've got a man at the wheel that knows his business, and has got his back up to get it done." (FS 77-8)

Duke lives in Tyler, Kathleen in Sardis, but she spends much of her time at the nearby Priest farm watching the drilling. She has to deal with the negativity of her mother-in-law: "Her eyes dark and set in deep sockets, held a perpetual spark of pain." (FS 81) With her sister-in-law, Ella, she discusses the merits of getting out of their so-limited existence, but Ella and her mother see no reason to even seek happiness. In contrast, Duke has a good understanding of this malaise and the austerity of their life, and he tells Kathleen how it's different from the ways of the oil people:

> "It's like the motto of the oilfields," Duke told Kathleen. "Get it. Get it done. It's like sloughing off all the 'ifs' and 'buts' you've been messing around with, all your life. Those big boys are big because they decide, and take chances, and do things. We people over here in the piney woods have just let things be done to us, for the last few generations. Once in a while I hear somebody—usually it's some of those newspaper fellows—talking a lot of bunk about turning a land of rural peace and contentment into 'just another oilfield.' But you're not peaceful and contented just because you live on a farm—we know that, Kats. Sometimes, when I jump into that old coupe on a bright morning, and go tearing out to a new location, it seems to me that the country itself is fairly rubbing its eyes. Part of that 'rustic quiet' they talk about was peace and contentment, I reckon; but a lot of it was just helplessness and hopelessness and stagnation." (FS 78-9)

Ella tells Kathleen that she is too nice and doesn't see the devilment in others. Then she gossips about Rose Anne, Cousin Harlowe's wife. The story as she gets it is that Rose Anne is throwing herself at Arkwright, one of the oil men who is drilling a well on Harlowe's farm. In addition, another oil man, Roy Vickery, a former suitor of Rose Anne, is chasing her. Then, she tells Kathleen about Cousin Fred, who has gone "hog-wild," using shyster tricks to get leases from his family and friends. Kathleen responds by commenting on what has changed in their lives because of the oil:

"What I mean is, a thing like that doesn't really change people, does it? Doesn't it just bring out what's already there? I've been thinking a lot about it, and it seems to me this isn't a different kind of life that's swooped down on us—it's just more of it in a lump. It's changed the scale of things, and speeded 'em up; but they're the same things. It seems a violent kind of life, because things that used to take ten years to happen, happen in a week. But they're the same sort of things that always happened."

"Rose Anne hasn't always carried on with other men."

"She couldn't carry on with old Brother Sykes and the cross-eyed boy that runs the filling-station, could she?"

"That's just what I've been saying," retorted Ella, the dull red beginning to show again on her high cheek-bones. "If all this hadn't come, she'd have gone along the rest of her days, quiet and contented."

"Quiet—maybe; but not contented. Do you really think people are good just because they never have a chance to go on a tear? That's what money does, it seems to me; it lets 'em get out everything that's in them. If they've managed to be happy when they were poor, they can be happy when they're rich; if they've been really good poor people, they can be good rich people. It's just opportunity: that's what it is. I don't see why anybody should be afraid of opportunity—unless he's afraid of himself." (FS 88)

Ella of course remains unconvinced. And Kathleen soon learns about some of Cousin Fred's devilment. She goes to the well where Uncle Fin, her mother-in-law's brother, is working as a night watchman. He tells her how Fred has deceived him in getting an oil lease on his property. Uncle Fin wants Kathleen to get Duke to talk to Fred about his problem. When Duke arrives, he is enraged because of Fred's dealings. He then tells Kathleen about how Fred has taken advantage of her old Sally:

> "I was over at Kerryville yesterday, sitting in my boat at a crossing waiting for a train to pass, when I heard somebody calling me. I realized I was sitting in front of old Sally's cabin; you know, it's right to the left of the main highway, where it crosses the tracks. Sure enough, she came hobbling out with a cane in each hand, looking like an old brown ghost. Seems she got knocked down by a truck about a month ago, and pretty well smashed up. Well, she had a long tale of woe about a good-looking white man who'd come to her house while she was flat on her back, and offered to pay her doctor-bill if she'd give him a lease on her place. Of course she did; she didn't know a lease from a barn-door. He told her all she had to do was to sign her name, so she did. Now things are warming up in Kerryville, and people are coming to her and offering big prices, every day. A man had just offered her two hundred and fifty. What she wanted me to do, was to see if I couldn't get the lease back some way, so

she could hold it for a bigger price." (*FS* 99)

The man who did this is, of course, Cousin Fred, and even though the doctor bill was only fifteen dollars, Fred asserts that it was a fair trade, and he won't consider changing it.

When Kathleen and Duke decide to visit Cousin Harlowe's well, we get a lyrical description of the East Texas countryside during the winter:

> It was a gray morning; not very cold, but with a raw bite in the air that always stirred Kathleen to a sense of adventure and romance. There were not many houses on the neighborhood roads that tacked across to Wellspring from the settlements around Sardis; but each little cabin or farmhouse flaunted a ragged plume of smoke, often star- tlingly blue against the black, encircling pines. There was something jolly about the way the wind snatched at the first puff from the chimney, and sent it scattering away across the fields as if pursued. (*FS* 103)

When they reach the well, Kathleen says that it is in the pine woods, which is the loveliest part of Harlowe's place. Duke tells her, "A fellow from Borger said to me yesterday that this was like an oilfield in a park." (*FS* 104) Then we get a description of the derricks, the pines, the people:

> A clearing had been made on the brink of a small ravine in the very heart of the pinewoods; tall pines stood all about it, and from the derrick floor the workmen looked down upon a sloping

green floor of brushy tops. The slender steel derrick soared past the treetops with an air of fragile
strength; great clouds of silvery steam blew shift-
ing patterns across it, and the ruddy flames under
the boilers glowed across the gray day like huge,
rude hearth-fires Most of the spectators about
the well were gathered in that quarter: sitting on
boxes or boards within the circle of warmth, or
standing with their hands behind them, spread
out to the blaze. A dozen cars of various sorts
and sizes were parked here and there among the
trees. (FS 105)

While there, Duke and Kathleen meet and like
Mr. Arkwright. He is a pleasant, well-dressed, highly educated, genteel easterner. He tells Kathleen
that Kerryville may be right in the middle of the oilfield. She sadly tells him that her family no longer
owns land there. Kathleen notices that Arkwright is
trying to avoid being around Rose Anne, Harlowe's
wife.

Kathleen tells Duke that if their well doesn't
come in, she will open a restaurant serving family-
style meals to the oil workers. They go to Kerryville
and discover that old Sally has already opened a
food business. Sally tells them how she got started:

"Well suh, I was out at de well a-drawin' a
bucket o' wawtah, an' all of a sudden I hyears
somebody a-callin', 'Hey, Auntie!' It was a real
young sort of a man that was a settin' right out
hyear whah you-all is, an' he was a-drivin' a truck
big's a box-cyar. I come to de gate, an' he say, 'I
smells coffee an' sausage.' Dat's jist what he say,

real fiercelike: 'I smells coffee an' sausage.' Den he laugh out loud an' say, sorta coaxin'-like, "What'll you take to bring me out some?'

"I looks him ovah an' I respon's, 'Oh, 'bout a dime, I reckon.'

"'A dime?' he says. 'Woman, you's a contortionist! I'se a po' wuckin' man, an' cain't pay dat much. Make it twobits—an' make it snappy. I cain't sit hyear all mawnin'. You hustle yo'se'f out hyere with a plate o' bread an' sausage an' a cup o' coffee. De slop in dat joint down de street ain't fit fo' a white man to eat.' An' it sho ain't, Mist' Duke; dat's de Lawd's truth."

Aunt Sally paused to enjoy one of the deep, noiseless chuckles of her kind. "Well, suh, dere was three others come up befo' he got through, an' I fed 'em all. Dey paid me two bits apiece an' I give 'em all dey could eat—jist sorta heaped t up, you know, comf'table-like. An' dat fust one, he say to me, 'Woman, you got de bes' stan' dis side o' Kilgore.' Now does you-all understan'?"

They understood

"You's got de bes' stan' dis side o' Kilgore,' he say. 'You jist sit hyere and thank de Lawd, an' keep de atmosphere disinfected good wid de smell o' sausage an' bacon,' he say. Well, suh, evah since, I sorta watches out fo' 'em an' tempts 'em, an' I'se fed some evah day. Dey woan come into a nig-gah-house to eat, but day sho will set outside an' eat what I brings 'em. No, suh, I doan want no oil-well a-tearin' up my gyardin. I jist wants my stan'." (FS 121-2)

Not long after this, Duke's father, Matt, becomes

seriously ill. Matt knows he is dying. He tells Duke not to stop the drilling of the well because of his death. Duke listens but doesn't promise. Soon Matt is dead, and the funeral is held, and the drilling is stopped.

Roy Vickery's well comes in. Roy is a hero — local boy makes good. There is still talk about him and Rose Anne, but she is too infatuated with Arkwright to pay much attention to him.

Then the Priest well comes in. While they are waiting two weeks for casing to be set, news reaches them that Harlowe's well is a dry hole. Because of Trumpler's poorboying the well, the Priest well is dangerous. First there is almost a serious accident:

> The plug had been drilled and the process of "washing" was well under way, when, about four o'clock, a shout went up from the derrick-floor that a cable was breaking. Miraculously, it thinned and spun itself out, but did not break: as a silk cord snaps, but holds together by a strand or two, sounder than the rest. Duke, who had been startled into the sharpest attention, wiped his forehead and drew a provisional breath of relief. "Blamed po' boy outfit!" he grumbled under his breath. "If it had let go altogether, it might have killed every man on the derrick. What in thunder Trumpler means, using stuff like that —" (FS 161-2)

The well comes in a gusher. Arkwright notices that Trumpler is shutting it off without checking the pressure first. Arkwright tells Duke to stay back to see if it holds. It does. So Arkwright relaxes and says, "Providence takes care of 'em—. sometimes. I've known it to be—otherwise." (FS 162) Before she goes to bed, Kathleen checks the well. Uncle Fin and his ward, Henry, are there and one member of the drilling crew. That night, they pay for Trumpler's slipshod ways — the well explodes:

> Without warning. Outrageously, incredibly. A roar that seemed to burst out of the silence like a beast out of a cave, filling the earth, the air, the sky. Then the leap of flame that followed the explosion. After that tongue of fire, a great burst of flame that roared and spread and mounted as if it were licking up the world. Great black billows of smoke like mountains, belching out as if all the inner fires were being disgorged at once. The whole roof of the sky was a gigantic rose, of deadly beauty. Duke, a grotesque figure in the wild light, leaped to his feet—then sat down again on the side of the bed, with the ashy face of despair. (FS 165)

Uncle Fin and the roughneck are killed, and Henry, who was at some distance from the well, has multiple injuries, including a broken leg. Mary Priest, already stressed by the death of her husband, loses her mind because of the event. She turns against Ella. She and Ella go to live with Uncle Fin's wife because their house is too close to the fire. Kathleen takes care of Henry. Efforts to put out the well are initially unsuccessful.

Trumpler is broke because of the explosion. In order to get money to fight the fire, the Priests need to make a deal with Arkwright to take over the well, but they can't because of Mary Priest's insanity. She must go before a hearing and be declared incompetent, but the young brother, Dave, won't agree to it at first. Finally reason prevails, and the deal is made, but still the well resists all attempts to put it out.

Meanwhile, Kathleen has had to face other adversities. Henry is depressed and emotionally distraught because of the explosion. Then, old Sally comes to Kathleen with news that some white men are trying to force her out of Kerryville and take over her stand. Kathleen gives up her teaching job and moves to Kerryville and opens up a restaurant at Sally's. Henry gets better immediately because Sally diverts him with her jokes and shenanigans. He also works at the restaurant as cashier. Sally cooks. Kathleen manages. It is an immediate success. Their sign reads: "AUNT SALLY'S CABIN, HOME-COOKED MEALS—FAMILY STYLE, K. KERRY PRIEST—MANAGER." (FS 194)

Kathleen begins to make enough money to buy up some oil leases in the area on the advice of Arkwright. Meanwhile, things are not going well at the Priest well fire. Expert after expert gives it a try. They are finally even considering a very expensive tunneling scheme. But Roy Vickery comes up with an idea for putting it out:

> "I don't know all about chemicals and tunneling, but I know about drag-lines. And I know that water won't burn. Now, say—look here." He had

an envelope out of his pocket, and was rapidly sketching a device upon it. "I've got the drag-line, and you've got that ten thousand barrel mud-hog pump. Look at this dinkus I've drawn here: they could make that in the shops at Kilgore in half a day. A tapering nipple, see, to fit into the top of the Christmas-tree. We can swing the water-line from the boom of a steam-shovel. The water's pumped into the tubing, and when the tubing's full it will come up on the outside, in the casting. There won't be any room for the fire, see? I'll bet a Stetson that'll put it out in sixty minutes, and won't cost but a few hundred dollars. That tunnel will cost thousands on top of thousands." (FS 203)

And it works. The fire is out within an hour of the time they begin work.

Shortly after this Kathleen discovers one day while Arkwright is eating at her restaurant that she loves him. It takes her completely by surprise. She is not happy about it either because she does not plan to act upon it:

> She could tell herself, with truth, that no woman had ever walked into it more unconsciously. She had always had, in relation to herself, a proud disdain of the mere idea of illicit love. In a woman like herself, she believed, who had had the normal experience of young love and passion; for whom marriage (though imperfect, like all things human) had ripened into a many-sided companionship and mutual dependence; who had had a child — in such a woman, it was a sign of immaturity to imagine that a succession of

love-affairs could supply what each separate one inevitably lacked. It was as if a child, gathering shells or bright pebbles, should continually throw away the one in hand, to pick up the brighter one the waves were still washing. She did not think lightly of love; all her life was a flowering, somewhere, of that spreading root. But to her love was the developed, human thing, in which passion is counterbalanced by affection and tenderness. And as for a love that could seize, like a disease or madness, upon a reasonable being who didn't want to be seized—that conception had always left her somewhat unconvinced. When she had run across it in books or in the talk of people, she had been halfconsciously skeptical. It seemed disingenuous and unreal. (*FS* 213)

Kathleen first considers running away, selling her restaurant, and avoiding Arkwright altogether. She decides that would be cowardly and unfair to Aunt Sally and her other employees. She soon has made lots of money in her business, and the Priest well is beginning to pay off. Then she discovers that Henry, who is an orphan, is the owner of land over the richest oil strike in the area. He is the richest of them all. After fending off the efforts of Fred to be made Henry's guardian, Kathleen and Arkwright become the guardians of Henry, Arkwright taking care of the business and Kathleen the education and family responsibilities. Henry hates school in Dallas because he is made fun of there because of his country way of talking. Kathleen continues to try to get him to pay more attention to his grammar.

One last tragic oilfield accident occurs. Roy Vickery has his hand caught in machinery on his well and through a long dangerous struggle manages to get free by having his hand amputated. Duke works to save him during the long struggle. Roy is apparently going to live, but in the hospital he contracts pneumonia and dies. Arkwright leaves. Kathleen sells the restaurant. Ella goes off to study to be a doctor. Duke gets involved in Kerryville government, and Kathleen and Duke buy the old brick mansion of her grandfather's and fix it up. The novel ends with them looking out from the house at the nearby oilfield. Duke thinks his view is a grandstand seat "at the greatest show on earth." (FS 307) And, proving that he still has grammar lessons to learn, Henry asks, "It is the biggest oilfield in the world sure enough, ain't it, Duke?" Then he says contentedly, "Gee, that's swell." (FS 307)

This is one of my favorite oilfield novels. The people seem real—good and bad, but not too good or bad. The events of the oilfield are described accurately and believably. It shows the varying ways one family has responded to the opportunities and dangers of life in the East Texas oilfield—the Priest family style.

Chapter 17

The Female Geologist

Twenty five years pass before there is another oil novel set in East Texas. The first of the two published in 1962, *The Young Texans* by Claude Garner has much in common with *Family Style*, having a female protagonist, important black characters, and a deceiving lease hound. The female protagonist, Jessie Bell, is only fourteen as the novel begins. She has just lost her parents, most recently her mother, who died in childbirth, leaving Jessie with a newly born sister, Paula, to care for. Fortunately, Jessie has a good friend, her black neighbor, Lilly White. Lilly has two children and is pregnant with another. Her oldest child, Ben Bob, is the child of her first husband killed in World War I. Ben Bob is a dependable young man, a successful farmer of the land they own. The second is Cathy, the daughter of her long-time white lover, Judge Rommum. Lilly is pregnant with the child of the deceptive lease hound, Tony Miles. She has never liked Tony, but he is a real smooth operator. He almost got her to sign a mineral deed instead of a lease. She had Rommum check the contract, and he caught the deception, so she receives a payment each year until a well is dug. Jessie thinks her mother had signed a lease with Miles, too. But she receives no payment. When she has the judge check, she discovers that Miles has cheated her mother by having her sign the mineral deed. She would never receive a penny whether or not oil was found on her land. Jessie hates Miles even more. She already had a grudge against him because he had tried to attack her sexually when he gave her a ride. She had fought him off and had never told anyone about it. Now she vows revenge. But first she has to worry about how she will be able to take care of Paula, her baby sister, and get the education that she knows that she needs.

The pastor of her Baptist church, Reverend Tolbert, is a kind, good man, and he provides an opportunity for her to accomplish her purposes. Earlier we have seen members of his congregation who are not so kind or good. Some are racially prejudiced, speaking of Lilly and Ben Bob as being "uppity." Reverend Tolbert finds employment for Jessie in the home of an oil-rich woman, Mary Morgan, who has recently moved into town and needs a young woman for a companion. The farm on which Mrs. Morgan has lived has been swallowed up by the worst part of the boom. Lilly knows the woman and likes her, saying, "She's good white folks —she's real quality — and Jessie could learn a lot from her." (YT37) Lilly agrees to continue to keep Paula. Mrs. Morgan will pay Jessie $20 a month, and her only responsibility will be to stay at home at night because Mrs. Morgan doesn't like to be alone then.

Because of overcrowding, Jessie is denied entrance into the school until Mrs. Morgan goes to talk to a member of the school board. Jessie has already been ambitious, but this further energizes her: "She now realized that there was not even equality of opportunity among whites, and of course Negroes were much worse than the poorest whites. But she had also seen, in action, the importance of wealth and influence, and she decided it would be wise to strive for these attributes, as well as for knowledge." (YT 44)

Jessie finishes her junior year with the highest grades in her school. She rents her house and land to Ben Bob to farm and uses the money to pay Lilly for taking care of Paula. Wopetco, Tony Miles' company, begins to drill on both Lilly's and Jessie's land, and she renews her vow to get revenge, even extending it to a distrust of all men. She tells her teacher, "I am not going to let anything or anybody wreck my life. But I never intend to trust any man. My mother trusted Tony Miles because she thought men were decent and honest like Papa." (YT 48)

However, she soon meets Dale Dawson, Mrs. Morgan's nephew. He is a petroleum engineering graduate of the University of Oklahoma. He is working in Shreveport with a geophysical exploration company doing seismographic work. She becomes fascinated by Dale and starts reading all about oil.

Lilly's well comes in producing several thousand barrels a day. And Lilly sees to it that Wopetco, Tony Miles's company, doesn't cheat her:

> "Mom sure made Wopetco pay off!" Ben Bob interrupted, beaming with admiration. "Ever since they started drilling out our way, them oilmen have run roughshod over the colored landowners. They drove heavy trucks and bulldozers

right across the fields and over the crops. They pushed roads to the well site and leveled an acre of land, then dug big, deep slush pits in the fields. And they wouldn't pay the landowners for the damage they had done to the land or the crops. But Mom put a stop to that! She made Wopetco pay off."

"More power to you, Lilly. I'll do the same thing if I ever get a chance."

"I didn't do it myself. I sicked my lawyerman on them. The Judge threatened to sue them and shut down all Wopetco's rigs if they didn't pay me five hundred dollars for damages. Before you could skin a cat, here comes Wopetco's landman with his checkbook. Then when they let the well blow oil on Ben Bob's cotton patch, I made them pay me three hundred dollars more for that." (YT 53)

The well on Jessie's land comes in flowing even stronger than Lilly's, so Jessie becomes even angrier about being cheated. Lilly sees to it that Jessie collects for damages to her property, so Jessie has money to go off to South Texas University in Houston. Lilly drives her there in Lilly's new Ford. After four days looking for a boarding house that will take Jessie and her two-year-old sister, Lilly suggests to Jessie that Lilly will buy a house and that they will set up their own high-class boarding house. Because Lilly will be unable to buy a house in a high-class neighborhood, Lilly puts up the money, and Jessie does the bargaining, and the house is put in Jessie's name. Once the semester starts, Lilly is able to fill the house with good dependable roomers, and her clientele for the tea room increases steadily. They also have quarters in garage apartments.

At first, because she is a woman, Jessie meets resistance in studying geology, but her grades, her recommendations, and a conversation with the dean convinces the registrar to allow her to take the courses she wants. So as a freshman, she takes paleontology and does well in it, so well that at the end of the year the dean offers her a summer job keeping a paleontology log. He explains the importance of the log to her:

> "Jessie, Texas has millions of acres of range land in West Texas, and timbered land in East Texas. Some of that land has oil possibilities. Our logging service is free, and it helps the state, individual landowners, oilmen, independent operators, and lease brokers. Then, too, we keep and file copies of each log made, and these give us valuable information on the earth beneath Texas. We are especially interested in the oil-bearing formations under the land around the wells we log. A good paleo log describes each formation penetrated by the bit while the well is being drilled, and this helps to evaluate other leases in the immediate area." (YT 93)

Jessie gets the job and succeeds at it even though she has to spend many hours looking into a high-powered microscope. She learns more from this job than she has in her whole first-year paleontology class.

During the next school year, she has a new professor, Jules Highbill. He is an outstanding teacher, and he becomes interested in her romantically. She is interested in him too, but when he proposes, she puts him off, saying that she could not even consider marriage until she graduates. He claims that Tony Miles and Wopetco have been responsible for his previous failures in oil. He still has influence with Wopetco, though, and he is able with the dean's help to get her a summer intern's job with them. He wants her to find information at Wopetco that they can use to drill wells for themselves. Dale Dawson comes to visit and proposes to her, and she accepts. Both Dale and Jules are expert in electric logs. Jessie learns from both of them and soon becomes more expert in electric and paleontological logs than most of the geologist working at Wopetco. She graduates and goes on to work on a master's in geology and a bachelor's in petroleum engineering.

Jessie's jobs and the profits from the boarding house have provided money to meet her and her sister Paula's expenses. Lilly has fallen in love with Harker Jeffers, a man who has helped remodel the rooming house. Lilly is reluctant to marry him because she wants her children to have all of her money. Jessie says she should ask Hark to sign a premarital waiver. So Lilly does and marries him with a big church wedding, attended by blacks and whites.

While running samples, Jessie finds something similar to what Jules Highbill was looking for. From her samples, she found two wells that had been plugged and abandoned. Both had great potential. She considers telling Highbill because he had asked her to look for such wells. But because he reminds her a little of Tony Miles, she holds back the information while getting his help:

> Instead, Jessie divided one batch of samples and put them in some old bags labeled from a well that was really dry. She then asked Jules to run the samples and see what he could find. Jules found the same saturation that she had discovered. Then, when he thought she was not looking, he copied the labels, unaware that she had switched bags and that the labels showed an inaccurate location. Thus, all they knew in common was that someone, through ignorance, carelessness, or deliberate intent, had passed up an oil well. She did not show Jules the samples from the other well, and only she knew where the wells were actually located. (YT 119)

Jessie becomes the first woman ever hired as a geologist by Wopetco. She works throughout the summer, making ever effort to be accepted by the other geologists, particularly Jim Pat Brown, for whom she is an assistant:

> Before the summer was over, Jim Pat had accepted Jessie as a competent critic; he was even flattered by her praise. She learned that compliments encouraged him to open up and talk about his findings, and together they studied the secret structural maps, highly confidential shooting information, and seismetic surveys in Wopetco's

general office. Jessie's photographic mind pictured every map so clearly that she could close her eyes and visualize each one again. (*YT* 124)

Dale comes to visit her at Christmas, and they spend most of their time talking about geology and oil. She is interested in what he tells her about what he has learned from seismetic surveys, particularly the counties in West Texas where he thinks there is oil. When she goes back to work for Wopetco the next summer, she quickly catches up on all of the logging she is expected to do and volunteers to do subsurface mapping of the fields in West Texas. Her boss' response to this is, she thinks, related to her being a woman:

> Later, as she reflected on his words, she realized that Jim Justin had not been the slightest bit suspicious of her motives because she was a woman. With this realization came the instinctive knowledge that her sex could be used as a powerful weapon if she did not waste it on feminine trivialities. Thus, in the days ahead, she went out of her way to make it clear that she intended to carry her share as if she had been a man, and that she expected no concessions on the grounds of her femininity; but in carrying out this endeavor, at no time did she attempt to talk or act like a man. If anything, she accentuated her femininity. The reaction of her male colleagues, as the days passed, was a mixture of wolf whistles and professional respect; she could not have asked for more. (*YT* 130)

The war in Europe begins, and Dale volunteers and uses his electrical expertise in working with fighter planes. Jessie graduates and is offered a job as a geologist. She accepts contingent on being assigned to the West Texas office, the one being managed by Tony Miles. She gets the job and is assigned to work with Pete Paulett, a nice older man, one with years of experience and extensive notebooks. He has had remarkable success finding oil using his vast knowledge of the geologic formations of the area. The office is in Center Plains, obviously a fictional version of Midland.

Lilly and her family decide to move with Jessie. They sell the rooming house at a profit, and upon arriving in Center Plains, buy two motels, one on the west of town and one on the east. The motels are new and demand for rooms is high, so they begin to make money on them immediately.

Jessie has trouble with Tony although he does not recognize her from East Texas. The lecherous Tony makes all of his usual moves, but Jessie will have nothing to do with him. She finds out from Pete that she only has to answer to Pete, so she avoids Tony whenever she can.

Dale is going off to the war, and he leaves all his seismographic records with her. She explains to Lilly what she found when she consulted them:

> "Don't you remember my showing you a paleo log that I made from samples I examined while I was working in the lab? I told you then that I'd found a well they had plugged as a dry hole that should have made a good producer? Lilly, that

well should make a good oil well."

"Yep, I remember all about that."

"I marked the location on my map, but I didn't tell a soul what I found. Here's a map Dale drew, and it shows there's an oilfield right where that old well was drilled."

"Now ain't that something! How in the world did Mr. Dale know there was an oilfield under that same land?"

"He located it when he made a seismic survey. I've wanted to buy that land ever since we moved out here. Now we just must buy it." (YT 154)

Jessie explains to Lilly that there are 1,280 acres of ranchland and that it is sitting on an oilfield. Jessie says that they should buy it and own the minerals and the royalty. She explains that Wopetco owns a ten-year lease that still has three years to run. After they buy the land, Jessie has a plan about how to get the lease away from Wopetco.

Ben Bob, Lilly's son is sent out to evaluate the ranch and to dicker with the owner about the price. The owner of the land, Mr. Tarplin, is eager to sell. He invested heavily in cattle with borrowed money and now he owes lots of money. Jessie and Lilly go in partners and buy the land using Ben Bob as the owner of record. Ben Bob and Lilly buy Tarplin's cattle, and Ben Bob and his wife move to the ranch to try to make it profitable pending the time they can get the lease and drill. Garner stops his novel's progress to write a miniature essay about the effect of oil on the ranchers of West Texas. (YT 161-2)

Jessie, out of a desire to get even with Tony and

Wopetco for stealing her oil, devises a scheme to get the leases. She has some compunction about her dishonesty but overcomes it: "The thought of having to double-cross Pete Paulett and Jim Justin was distasteful, but she reminded herself that soft-ness, weakness, and sentiment had no place in the oil business." (YT 161) She has been offered other jobs at higher pay, but she will stay with Wopetco until she can get the Tarplin lease of 1280 acres and the Swartz lease of 860, both of which she believes are potential oilfields.

Jessie's scheme is to see to it that the annual rental payment on the Tarplin lease is not made, so that the lease will be ended by default. She knows that each month Tony Miles staples onto each lease's file jacket instructions about which leases are to be renewed and which are to be allowed to lapse. After the secretary leaves, Jessie goes in and unstaples the instructions and switches them, being careful to restaple them using the same holes. The narra-tor tells us, "Jessie did not regret her dishonesty. She felt justified in doing what she had done." (YT 162) January fifteenth passes, and Jessie knows that she has got away with it. Wopetco no longer has a lease on their land.

Dale is sent overseas, and Jules comes by to try to seduce her, but she is able to withstand his charms. She also discovers that Jules had lied to her about Tony Miles being responsible for his first failure in the oil business. She is glad she has never trusted him with any of the confidential informa-tion she has had.

Then comes Pearl Harbor with the subsequent loss, through enlistments, of many of the field geologists. She has previously only worked as a geologist in the office, but she goes into the field to supervise drilling operations and is quite successful. She makes friends with one of Wopetco's drillers, Stanley Duncan, who comes to have great respect for her even though he distrusted a female geologist at first.

Jessie also manipulates the papers to get the Schwarz lease. Ben Bob buys the land for her and Lilly. Pete has a heart attack and dies at his desk, so Lilly becomes the chief geologist and continues to work in the field until the war is over. When it is, she resigns, saying that it is to give the men returning from the war a chance to get jobs. Actually, she and Lilly are ready to start drilling the two leases. She hires Stanley Duncan to drill for her. She doesn't drill where the previous well was because she wants to drill next to Wopetco land so that they will pay bottom-hole money to her. They agree to, but at first Tony won't pay the money, having put in a clause in the contract which he thinks will keep her from getting the money. He says that if she will fool around with him, he will see that the company pays her. She tapes him saying this and forces him to pay. She also tells him who she and Lilly are. They stop drilling thinking the well is a dry hole. Actually, she just hasn't drilled deeply enough. She consults the notes of Pete and discovers why this hole is dry. She drills in the proper place, and this time she is able to see early that it will be a producing well. She shuts down operation until she can buy more land nearby. Finally the well comes in as an excellent producer. In order to drill more wells, she must either borrow money or take in partners. Jules helps her secure a partner, Mr. Gunn. She tapes Jules and Gunn talking and discovers that Jules believes that there is a possibility of wells on this lease producing at more than one level. Jules thinks Jessie stopped too soon on the first well. She consults Dale's logs and Pete's notes, and she sees that Jules is right. She does form a partnership with Gunn, and they soon are making lots of money. She has difficulty with Tony one final time over an agreement with Wopetco in digging a test well on the Schwarz property.

Dale comes to town briefly. He is on his way back to Europe and wants Jessie to marry him and go with him. She refuses since her wells are at such a critical stage of development. They almost break up, but he comes back briefly, and they are married. She continues to have success after success. She builds an empire. She stoops to lying and junking wells, but she ultimately succeeds. She names a field after Dale.

When Dale returns, she thinks he will be proud of her for what she has accomplished. But he isn't. His pride seems to be wounded because a woman has succeeded so well. Lilly joins in condemning her for her behavior, explaining to Dale why she and Jessie had been fighting:

"Money—money—money," replied Lilly,

singing it off. "Jessie can spend money faster than Uncle Sam can print it. Now I didn't mind her spendin' over a half-million dollars of my own money and it was all right for her to use our royalty money. And I didn't mind her spending all that money she got from Mr. Gunn and that Mr. Kiznar. But when she tried to make me sign a note and mortgage our oil-run money, so she could borrow a big wad of money from the bank — Mr. Dale, right there I balked." *(YT 280)*

Jessie has not been spending the money but successfully investing it. But Dale agrees with Lilly that drilling oil wells with borrowed money is dangerous business, especially wildcats. He says it is wise to let your oil income pay for drilling the field wells. Lilly wants Dale to take the stock they have given him and join it with hers to take control of the company. Dale won't do it, insisting that Jessie should keep running it. Lilly says no, "I ain't goin' to let Jessie run that business like she wants to run it. She's a natural-born schemer, and she won't let nobody tell her what to do, but she'll tell the other fellow what to do." *(YT 280)*

Dale refuses to get mixed up in their argument. He says they should sell the business or one should buy the other out. Lilly won't and says Jessie knows how she feels and knows that Lilly is right. They express their love for each other. Then Dale comments on their friendship:

"In my travels around the world, I've seen so much prejudice and hatred among the different races that I've often wondered if there was an answer. Then I would think about Jessie Bell and Lilly White, who have shown that whites and Negroes of the Deep South can live in peace, work in harmony, and help each other as they go through life." (*YT* 280)

Lilly says that she wants to keep on doing that and that she is the same but that Jessie has changed: "She ain't the same sweet girl she was when you fell in love with her back in East Texas." (*YT* 281) Jessie denies it. Then Lilly tells Dale that Jessie still loves him. Dale agrees but says that Jessie has changed: "But out here, she's a different person; there are times when she seems a stranger, a scheming career woman a hard, ruthless oil woman, a grasping and domineering business woman. There are times when the change frightens me — and makes me wonder if we're right for each other." (*YT* 281)

Lilly says it's too late to worry about that now because they are already married. Lilly believes she knows what motivated Jessie to become so scheming: "She didn't want to lose the man she loved, so she started fighting the best way she could. Jessie figured that she could hold you if she found lots of oil and built a big business that would be big enough to hold you. Deep down in her heart, Jessie ain't no business woman, but she figured she'd become one, if that's what it took to hold the man she loved." (*YT* 281)

Dale says that he didn't expect her to and that he could support her. The narrator reports that Jessie is surprised and pleased by all of this. Lilly says Jessie wanted to have something more than herself when he returned: "So if Jessie's mean and hard and bossy at times — and Lord only knows she is — it's because she's had to fight to hold her own in the oil business. She's had to fight to get back at the world — and some of the low people in it — for what they done to her. But deep down inside, Jessie is pure woman, and that means that she ain't much different from all the rest of us women. All she wants is a man — her own man — to guide and protect her." (YT 282-33) This is the big scene. After this, Jessie has Dale sell out all her holdings to Wopetco for $31,000,000 in stock. He becomes a vice-president and member of the board of directors. She gets pregnant and plans to stay at home and raise a family.

For 1962, this may have seemed like an appropriate ending, but now it seems an inappropriate and silly one. The author has Lilly — who refused to give her husband any say in her finances — be the mouthpiece for this view of what a woman's role is. Why has Jessie's success as geologist, engineer, and entrepreneur been given such treatment? Why has Jessie fought so hard to get an education? Was it just to impress Dale? Nothing earlier in the novel suggests this. The ending just doesn't fit with the characterization of the rest of the book. It was an interesting, well-written novel until the end. It's too bad that Garner chose such an old-fashioned set of values to espouse here at the end. I can see Jessie having a family, being a wife, and continuing to be active in her profession. I can not see the character created here, just giving up her profession.

Chapter 18

Slant Hole Drilling

Like *The Young Texans*, the next oil novel, Robert Roark's *Drill a Crooked Hole* (1968), begins in East Texas and ends up in West Texas. This is a three part novel, the first part covering the early stages of the slant hole drilling beginning in 1948. This is one of those novels where the narrator is a secondary character who reports what the more important character has done. Tom Kirk is the reporter. In fact, he is the newly appointed, oil editor for the Houston *Star Herald*. He arrives in East Texas in response to a tip that one Johnny Bratton would soon be making an important oil strike. He is quick to learn that the well is being drilled by Kelly Mason, a driller already well known as a specialist in deviational drilling. From this practice comes the title, *Drill a Crooked Hole*. Kirk is a likeable, relatively unambitious fellow, who gets along well with the locals and learns quickly that he is not too welcome by Bratton and his wife at the drilling site. He learns a lot about Bratton, who has been up to this time called "Dry Hole Johnny." Johnny's father, Jim Bratton, had been a legend in the oilfield, making great strikes in Mexia and East Texas, but also losing much of what he made through other wildcatting efforts. In 1931, it looked as if he had finally made it really big, but when the Rangers and

National Guard came in and the field was closed, he had been forced to sell off his holdings at a small part of their value because of money he owed for developing his field. He tried to make one more start and was drilling a well in South Texas when a drill string stuck. He had put all the power possible into pulling it loose, but the line had broken, bringing the crown block down upon him, killing him instantly. Johnny had sworn never to get into the oil business. But when he returns from World War II, he does start wildcatting. He drills dry hole after dry hole. His wife, the daughter of a doctor, takes a job and supports the family. There is no explanation of how he finances his wildcatting failures. But before his last dry hole, an executive of National Oil had agreed to provide dry hole money for the test well. Then the upper management, primarily the president, James T Fincher, welched on the deal.

So now Johnny has joined with Mike Henderson to drill a well next to National Oils' lease into a pool of National oil. Mike Henderson has a grudge against Fincher, too. Mike had been in love with Fincher's daughter. Fincher had tried to keep his daughter from marrying Mike. She was going to marry Mike anyway, but Mike had to leave with the marines for the Pacific. She died in child birth, leaving Mike's child. Mike was wounded in battle and returned bearing a grudge for Fincher. The child thinks Mike is his uncle. Big Mike is a hard drinking, fast living, self-made lawyer and oil man.

Kirk meets and comes to know well these, and several other interesting characters. There is Lela, the black maid, who has been with the Bratton family through all the ups and downs over the many years. She serves as a kind of chorus, telling Johnny of the dangers of wildcatting. There is H. L. King, better known as "Hard Luck." Johnny, after his last dry hole in South East Texas while driving home, had seen a black child run across the road before him. He tried to rescue the child and return him to his parents but discovered that the boy was an orphan and no one would take him in. So Johnny brought him home. His wife accepted responsibility for the child even though he was another mouth to feed, and they were extremely short on cash.

Another pair of interesting characters, who are friends of Johnny, are Mattie Lumpkin and Waldo Deschields. Mattie is the former madam and owner of the Blue Gander. Waldo is a Harvard educated aristocrat who came to Texas during the boom. He lost his money when the field was shut down. He stayed around and worked in the oilfield and became an alcoholic.

Kirk meets all of these people when he comes to cover his first oil story. When Johnny's well comes in, it is obviously flowing a great quantity of oil, but he tells Kirk that for his story he should report that it is producing seventy six barrels an hour on a pump. Kirk knows that Johnny is lying, but he goes along with the owner's report because he does not think that it is his job to break the story of East Texas deviational drilling because it is obvious that the big oil companies know about it and are choosing to overlook it for their own economic reasons.

It is also clear to Kirk that Mrs. Bratton and the Bratton's friends, Bob and Betty Harcourt, don't approve of the deviational drilling. Bob is also an unsuccessful wildcatter.

Part two of the book covers the years from 1956-62. Kirk sees Johnny growing increasingly rich. We see examples of conspicuous consumption and benevolence. Johnny builds a huge house. He contributes to orphan homes and the church. He joins with others in a weekend trip by train to the Kentucky Derby. Kirk even goes along. On the train, Kirk hears rumors that National and the other major oil companies are going to close down the illegal drilling. Johnny and Mike do not seem much concerned, but they continue to seek legal production and have some successes and failures in doing so. In 1962, Fincher and the other majors have their man as attorney general, and they move on those doing the deviational drilling. Mike and Johnny are closed up, brought to court, forced to pay fines and restitution, and are ultimately bankrupted and forced out of business. Even before all of this, Johnny's wife dies suddenly of a heart attack. His friend, Bob Harcourt, is also killed in a drilling accident. Johnny is at a low point in his life, and he takes to drinking heavily.

The oil business in East Texas during this time is in almost as bad a shape as is Johnny:

> By mid-April Star Sanders, the Kilview show-off of the Derby trip, had sold his last Cadillac and was looking for a job. But nobody would hire

him, so precise Daisyetta went to work in a dress shop. "Joe boy" Riddle faced disbarment as well as a charge of perjury. One by one the members of the fraternity fell under the inexorable hammer that continued to swing in the courts of East Texas.

Nor were the men who once laughed and joked about their deviated wells the only ones hurt. The people of Longton, Kilview, and other towns in the oil patch who had at first felt no real sense of participation in the catastrophe found themselves caught up in a serious economic slump.

Over one thousand oil wells had been shut down by the Texas Rangers on orders from the Railroad Commission, resulting in an annual loss of around $25,000,000. Also more than 150 oil operators were tied up in the courts and were unable to produce a drop of oil. Their employees, as well as royalty owners, small contractors, supply house workers, truckers, and others in the field were feeling the pinch of unemployment forced on them by the major oil companies. They were resentful, angry.

Merchants, churches, and schools suffered. Local banks were hurt by loans they could not collect, as were banks in Dallas and Houston which had made huge loans to the oil operators. There was a loss in taxes to county, state, and federal governments. (DCH 247)

To top off all this sad news, Kirk learns that Big Mike has tuberculosis and is in the hospital in Kerrville. Part two ends on this sad note.

Part three begins in May of 1965. Kirk gets a

call from Betty Harcourt inviting him to East Texas for a business conference. He goes because he has always been infatuated with her, and now she is a widow. When Kirk gets there he discovers that Johnny has managed to get a lease in West Texas. He has been unable to get any financing, but he has invited several of his friends to a meeting— Waldo, Mattie, Kelly, Hard Luck, Betty, Kirk, and Jake Ennis, paroled hijacker. He tells them about the dry land lease in West Texas he has secured from an old rancher, Asa Scott. He says of Asa: "He's short, squat, and spry. Red as a Comanche, has eyes that'll drill right through a man. So you'd better tell him the truth." (DCH 260)

Johnny had secured seismographic information from Jim Laster, a former employee and now seismograph interpreter for National. Laster had slipped him a map with the true shot points on it. Johnny has told Asa Scott his troubles: "I don't know why I'm sitting here thinking about a well that'll cost from ninety to one hundred and twenty thousand dollars to see the sand. Can't sell it unless I've got a lease and can't lease it because I'm broke." (DCH 261) Asa comments, "Boy, you're in one more God damn hell of a fix." (DCH 261) Finally Asa agrees to give him an eighteen-month free lease.

After telling the group that he got the free lease, he offers them each a one-thirty-second in the deal if they will help him drill it. They will be the crew, and he will still have to figure out how to get the rig and pipe that he will need. Much of the rest of the novel is about all the shenanigans the group pulls in order to get the well drilled. They lie, steal, cajole. They have troubles — twist-offs and fishing expeditions. Once Johnny has to push the rig to the maximum, and his friends remember how Johnny's father was killed. There is a friendly Sheriff, who helps. He is a former war buddy of Big Mike. There is a deputy sheriff, who causes trouble. He is a former sadistic prison guard, who mistreated Jake Ennis while he was in prison. So a bare knuckle fight is arranged between the deputy and Jake. It is a brutal affair with Jake the probable winner, but both end up in the hospital. This delays their work since Jake is one of the drillers. Work is delayed too when Johnny has to go to Big Mike's bedside and then his funeral. While there, he discovers he loves Betty. In the big final scene, Betty arrives just in time to see the well come in.

This novel is much like *Honor at Daybreak* in describing a group of friends working on a rig together with great difficulty and without much hope of success. In both cases the crew is of mixed race, but its members cooperate for the success of the venture. Like almost every oil novel, it has a raging well fire, but this one is distinctive in that it was extinguished by Red Adair.

Chapter 19

Leela

In *Drill a Crooked Hole*, the black character, Hard Luck, has an important role, but it is minor in contrast to that of the black characters in Anita Richmond Bunkley's *Black Gold* (1994). Set in Mexia, the novel has a female black protagonist, Leela Alexander. She is deeply involved in the discovery of oil, and this part of her life is fully covered, but the novel focuses more on the family relations of Leela, which are quite complicated. The novel begins when Leela is a child. Her father is a cook on the railroad. Her mother died in childbirth. Leela stays at home with her strange African grandmother, Ekkiti. Ekkiti is a "spirit calling soothsayer" who practices voodoo. While on one of his trips, Leela's father, Ed Brannon, meets a woman, Hattie Logan, near Waco. He falls in love with her, has sex with her, and plans to see her again. But on the same trip, he dies in a fire in his galley. Hattie already has a child, T. J., by a former husband and then she has Ed's child. She sends the older boy to work as day labor for his keep on a white man's farm near Mexia. She keeps Ed's child, Carey, near her and over the years spoils him as best she can on her meager subsistence salary as a janitor and washer woman.

Meanwhile, Leela has grown unhappily to a young teenager with her grandmother. When Ekkiti dies, Leela goes to live with her father's sister, Effie, and takes their name, Alexander. She loves her Aunt Effie and her cousin Parker, and they love her. But from the first her cousin Josephine is jealous of her and resents her. Parker, an older teenager, works for a black newspaper. When whites, protesting a story, throw a rock through the window of the newspaper office, Parker throws it back out. One of the mob claims that the rock hit him, and Parker is arrested on the trumped-up charges. Leela tries to defend him and just makes matters worse. Money is raised for Parker to pay his fine, and he leaves for Chicago, where he will take a job on a newspaper.

Leela remains in Mexia relatively happy with her new family until she meets a local farmer, T. J. Logan. At first, T. J. had suffered a great deal on the farm and wondered why his mother had sent him off to live such a painful lonely life. But he had worked hard, and finally his white owner had taken him in to his house and had willed the entire farm to T. J.. After the farmer's death, T. J. had made a success of the farm, but he has not let his mother come to live with him there. She still spoils Carey even though Carey has turned out to be a charming ne'er-do-well, who cuts school, gambles, fights, and drinks. After a squabble with his mother and T. J., Carey leaves home to make his way as a gambler, forger, and con man.

Leela and T. J. fall in love and are married. Things go well for a while as T. J. borrows money from the bank and expands his farm. She has a child, Kenny, and life goes well with her. Meanwhile, her cousin Josephine is living a disastrous life. She has two children that she neglects. Their father beats her, and she drinks to forget her miserable life.

Leela's life is disturbed when Carey arrives at their farm wounded from a cutting scrape. T. J. allows him to stay until he recuperates. While there, Carey tries to seduce Leela. She is momentarily tempted by Carey's charm, but about to resist him, when T. J. arrives. He throws Carey off the farm and tells him not to return.

For seven more years T. J. and Leela live together but never in the same trusting relationship as before. Then T. J. contracts tuberculosis and begins to waste away. He can't plant cotton, so they plant beans and melons, and Leela works in the field while T. J. lies sick in bed. A $3,000 payment has been missed in January, but their banker, Wesley Sparks, has said the payment can be made in the fall after the crops are all in. Then oil is discovered in the area, and Mr. Sparks comes to say that the payment will have to be made in thirty days. T. J. dies not knowing of the financial crisis. She has enough watermelons in the field to pay off the mortgage, but then she will have nothing to live on.

Leela stops by to see her Aunt Effie on the way to the bank to discuss the loan. She tells Effie about the trouble she is having with Sparks. Effie is surprised because Sparks had always been upright in his dealings with them. Then Leela explains the complicating factor:

"Not when there's talk of oil," Leela began, going on to tell Effie of her conversation with Wesley Sparks and of the test well being drilled on the Rogers place. Effie grinned and nodded her head at the news.

"I was born seventy-two years ago, exactly two miles from your farm. That sticky black stuff showed up all through that area back then—you know that's why they named that area Rioluces. My momma and others who knew how to do it used to scrape that black slimy stuff up off the river bank and burn it. I can still remember the smell. Strong and smoky. Stayed in your clothes for weeks. Most folks thought it a nuisance. Horses and cows wouldn't drink from the creek, and superstitious folks thought the water was cursed. I always figured somebody would sink enough money into that land to bring up oil in my lifetime. Bet Wesley Sparks and those men at the bank know more than they're telling you." (BIG 191)

Leela agrees with her, and then Effie tells her about a black man who is drilling oil wells, Victor Beaufort. He has told Effie that he is from Oklahoma and is looking for land to lease. Effie says, "I never heard tell of a colored man talking oil before." (BIG 191) Then she tells Leela to go by and see him. Effie also warns Leela about signing papers unless she has a lawyer look at them.

When Leela reaches the bank and asks for Wesley Sparks, a rude clerk tells her that he is not there. Then the clerk asks her what business she has with him. She tells the clerk it's about a loan, and the clerk says that they don't make loans to colored people. She says that she already has a loan. After more rudeness, she is allowed to speak to the bank manager, Mr. Barnard. Mr. Barnard explains to her that Wesley Sparks has vanished, absconding with bank funds. He also speaks rudely to her, insisting that they would never have loaned money to "Negroes" and that he was surprised that Sparks had. He agreed to look at her watermelon crop and decide whether or not to give her an extension. That night a tornado hits her farm and destroys her whole crop.

So Leela goes to see Victor Beaufort about leasing her land. She is disappointed when he tells her that it would lease for as little as ten cents an acre and as much as a dollar. She asks him how long it would take to bring in a well. She explains to him that she needs $3,000 right away. After the storm the bank examiner never came, and she hasn't been willing to face Mr. Barnard again. Beaufort tells her that there is no way she can get more than $500 for a lease right then. Later she might be able to get more.

Nevertheless, he says that he wants to see her land and that maybe they can work something out. Leela begins to feel a strong attraction to him. He comes to see her land and is at first very cautious. She asks him about his experience in the oil business. He tells her about how he got started:

> My brothers and I were oilfield orphans, never did know who our parents were. A Cherokee

woman named Annie Bowlegs kind of raised us. She was a field cook at the drilling site. So the white men in the oilfields knew us. First job I ever had was carrying water from derrick to derrick at Red Fork. Twenty-five cents a day from sunup to sundown. And I loved it. (*BIG* 219)

Victor tells her how life is in the oilfield for a black man:

You must understand one thing. The oil business has no place for black men. Even in the fields, digging ditches, pushing pipe, my brothers and I rarely saw another black face. We grew up in the shadows of the derricks of Tulsa when the Sue Bland well came in at Red Fork. We played hide-and-seek between red-hot boilers and built ant farms at the foot of wooden storage tanks. (*BIG* 219)

He tells her how he managed in the field:

My two brothers and I started out in the oilfields digging ditches and laying pipe. You were right, I worked the Osage fields, some of the most productive in the state. But I got no profits from that oil, only two dollars a day as long as my hands and my back held out, and only if the gang pusher was willing to tolerate a colored man on his team. Some were more agreeable than others.

We got to be pretty well known on the drilling circuits," Victor continued "A good word from a former boss man helped us get jobs. But we were the exceptions and it's still that way. Looking for oil requires money, trust and a common bond between men willing to rely on a handshake deal . . . and I don't know any white man who feels comfortable doing that kind of business with a colored man. I think my chances are better in a place like this. (BIG 219)

He then explains how Mexia is different because of the land owned by blacks. And he tells her how he and his brothers got money together to buy leases:

It was dirty work but there was a lot of it, so my brothers, Cap and Frank, and I just went from gang to gang over the area. Wherever we could hire on is where we stayed. But we had bigger ideas and eventually pooled our wages to buy up a load of rusted pipe. We cut and retooled the pipe and sold it to an oil company for four times what we paid for it. That got us hooked, and there was no way we would ever go back to digging ditches after that. Our little pipe company has done so well we've got enough money to buy up a few leases, and I want to try my luck at wildcatting. (BIG 219)

Shortly after this conversation, Leela is discouraged, thinking that she will lose her land. Then her horse runs away. In the action that follows she steps into a mire, and they discover on her feet — oil. Of course, oil on the surface does not mean that there is oil deep below the surface, but they are impressed by it, and Victor decides to lease her land. He convinces the bank that there is no oil on her land. Then when a nearby well comes in, the price of leases goes up. He sells one of his leases at a profit, pays off her land, signs a lease with her, and prepares to drill.

Things move fast after this. Victor and she fall in love. He has difficulty getting supplies, probably because he is black. Finally, though, the well comes in a gusher. He drills others. He is harassed until he hires armed guards to protect the wells. In spite of this there is an explosion, and Victor is having difficulty fulfilling a contract he was suckered into by Mr. Thornton Welch of Starr Oil as the following conversation shows:

> "That's a pretty tough bargain you're trying to strike," he said bluntly, not at all happy with the deal he'd just been offered.
>
> "I think it's a fair approach, Mr. Beaufort. We need each other and this way we both profit. Without Starr Oil piping your crude out of the ground and shipping it to the refinery in Corsicana, what do you really have, Mr. Beaufort? Nothing but a sump full of crude that will deteriorate daily. Subject to fires and contamination, too. Not a very good way to store oil."
>
> "That's not news," Victor replied glumly. "Why else do you think I agreed to our original deal? Rioluces Number 1 came in so big and so fast I was glad to sign up with you. And Number 2 is holding its own, though I know production might be slipping a little. But eighty-five percent? I'm sorry, Mr. Welch, that's a big chunk of my lease on Rioluces."
>
> "I don't think so. Not when you stand to lose the entire lease unless production increases substantially. With all due respect, Mr. Beaufort, you know the terms of our contract. Based on

your projections you guaranteed production of 750,000 barrels of oil by the end of the year. Rioluces Number 1 has fallen from 5,000 to 2,500 barrels a day. Number 2 is declining steadily and you've got a ways to go on Number 3. The way it looks, unless Number 3 comes in big and we can get production out of it very quickly, you're not going to make the terms of your contract." *(BIG 275)*

Embarrassed by his financial woes, Victor refuses to tell Leela of his troubles, and then things get worse when T. J.'s brother, the rascally Carey returns. He is a master forger and has forged a letter from his brother, saying that Carey should look after Leela and that the farm was as much Carey's as his. Leela will have nothing to do with Carey and drives him out.

Victor has been unsuccessful in raising money to help him finish the Number 3 well. So he falls prey to a scheme by Carey. Carey has enough money to buy five percent of Victor's stake in the drilling company. He then takes the paper assigning him the five percent and alters it before selling off many shares of worthless stock. When the people discover they have been swindled, they come to the farm and destroy it and the wells. Leela holds Victor responsible and says that she never wants to see him again. Meanwhile, Hattie has figured out that Leela and Carey are both Ed Brannon's children. She tells Carey about it just before she has a stroke. When Leela comes looking for Carey, he is drunk in the same house with Leela's drunken bootlegging cousin, Jacqueline. Carey pulls a gun on Leela. She struggles. He is killed. Jacqueline, still hating Leela, tells the sheriff that Leela killed him intentionally. During the trial, a witness is found to clear Leela. Victor sticks by her through the trial, and in the end they reconcile and vow to love forever.

The oilfield around Mexia was never as large as that around Kilgore, but it was one in which oil land was sometimes owned by poor black farmers. From the first East Texas oil fiction by Winifred Sanford in 1931 to the last by Bunkley, Blacks play an important part. Only in Bunkley's novel do we see a Black leading in the discovery, drilling, and producing of oil. In Roark's novel, Hard Luck works on the rig in West Texas but does not play a major role. Lilly in *The Young Texans* is a successful Black owner of oil wells. She is astute in her own right, but she is helped by Jessie's expertise. In *Family Style*, old Sally, aided by Kathleen Priest, makes a good living at her "stand."

Appendix 1

Works Cited

Baker, Karle Wilson. *Family Style*. New York: Coward-McCann, Inc., 1937.

Beach, Rex. *Flowing Gold*. New York: Harper & Brothers, 1922.

Bunkley, Anita Richmond. *Black Gold*. New York: Dutton, 1994.

Daniels, Gertrude Potter. *Eshek the Oppressor*. Chicago: Madison Book Company, 1902.

Garner, Claud. *The Young Texans*. New York: Signet Paperback, 1962.

Gibson, Jewel. *Black Gold*. New York: Random House, 1950.

Gilkyson, Walter. Oil. Chicago: The White House,1924.

Kelton, Elmer. *Honor At Daybreak*. New York: Doubleday, 1991.

-----. *The Man Who Rode Midnight*. New York: Doubleday,1987

King, Mary. *Quincie Bolliver*. Boston: Houghton Mifflin, 1941.

Logan, Chauncey. *Burkburnett*. San Antonio: The

Naylor Co., 1973.

Owens, William A. *Fever in the Earth*. New York: G.P. Putnam's Sons, 1958.

Oyen, Henry. *Tarrant of Tin Spout*. New York: George H. Doran Company, 1922.

Patterson, Norma and Crate Dalton. *Out of the Ground*. New York: Farrar & Rinehart,1937.

Pendleton, Tom. *The Iron Orchard*. New York: McGraw Hill, 1966.

Ragsdale, Clyde B. *The Big Fist*. New York: G.P. Putnam's Sons, 1950.

Raine, William MacLeod. *Gunsight Pass How Oil Came to the Cattle Country and Brought the New West* . Boston: Houghton Mifflin, 1921.

Rangeler, Harry. *Silenced by Gold, The Story of a Wildcat Well*. New York: The Abbey Press, 1902.

Rex Beach. *Flowing Gold*. New York: Harper & Brothers, 1922.

Rickman, J. C. *Racing Bits A Story of the Oil-Fields of Texas*. Boston: Richard G. Badger, 1926.

Roark, Garland. *Drill a Crooked Hole*. Garden City, New York: Doubleday & Co., 1968.

Sanders, Leonard. *Fort Worth*. New York: Delacorte Press,1984.

Sanford, Winifred M. *Windfall and Other Stories*. Dallas: Southern Methodist University Press, 1980.

Thompson, Cole. *Chocolate Lizards*. New York: St Martin's Press, 1999.

Walker, Jack. *Boomer's Gold*. Berkeley, California and Amarillo, Texas: Thorp Springs Press, 1978.

Appendix 2

Other Texas Oilfield Novels

For various reasons I decided not to include the following books in my main text. Some were not well-written. Most were not sufficiently about discovery and production, only about people who had oil-money or jobs in the oil business.

Bass, Rick. *Where the Sea Used to Be*. Houghton Mifflin:Boston, New York., 1998

Old Dudley, a rich wildcatter, sends his young geologist, Wallis, to Montana to find oil. Dudley's daughter, xxx, lives in Swan Valley in far northern Montana. Wallis and XXX become lovers. Following Wallis' recommendations Dudley begins drilling a well during the summer. A fire drives the drilling crew from the valley. Old Dudley with his other geologist, Matthews, arrives during the fire. Dudley, recalling his experience in the oil field fifty years earlier, puts his two geologist to work drilling. Matthews falls from the derrick and is wounded by a dirty screw driver. As winter comes the fires stop and the crew returns. Wallis and Matthews go on an extended Elk hunt for needed winter meat. When they return, Dudley informs them that he has reached 18,000 feet and that they have a dry hole. Dudley then starts home, but is lost in a snow storm. He is found, but they are not able to keep him alive.

Dudley is one of the most disagreeable, unpleasant, and obstreperous oil man in any oil novel. The Old Man in Sinclair's *Oil!* is nice compared to him.

Bean, Fred. *Black Gold*. New York: Forge, 1997.

This is about Texas Rangers fighting a New York mob for the control of the East Texas oilfield. It's about law enforcement in the oilfield, not about the production of oil. It's a well-done adventure tale.

Bryan, J. P. *Gordon Reed*. Austin and New York: The Pemberton Press, 1968.

This is a biographical novel covering the life of Gordon Reed. There is a lot here about the oil business particularly one large deal on the South Texas coast, but it is not good fiction.

Catto, Max. *King Oil*. New York: Simon and Schuster, 1970.

King Oil is the most unbelievable oil novel ever written. If you know anything about West Texas history or oil drilling, you can get a lot of laughs out of this one. In the 1880s, the rancher hero gets dynamite from a West Texas mine, puts it in a wagon, drives it in the general direction of an oil fire before cutting the wagon loose from the horses. This stratagem remarkably puts out the fire. Then he covers the well with dirt to keep the oil in.

Clark, Laverne Harrell. *Keepers Of the Earth*. El Paso, Texas: Cinco Puntos Press: 1996.

This is a novel of family relationships set in Central Texas in the sixties. An unsuccesful attempt is made at drilling for oil.

Fall, Thomas. *The Profit and the Loss*. New York: David McKay Company Inc., 1965.

This is a family conflict novel set on the Texas coast. Oil holdings come into play.

Ferber, Edna. *Giant*. Doubleday: New York, 1952.

Most people think this is an oil novel, but there is almost nothing about oil in it. Jett Rink tells Leslie that he and his uncle are drilling for oil. How he learned about drilling is never explained. Later he gets in a fight with Bick after he strikes oil. Somehow he becomes super rich, but there is no other explanation about how. Mostly the novel traces his eccentricities, drunkenness, and boorish behavior. The movie is better, but even it deals little with oil.

Goyen, William. *Come the Restorer*. Garden City, New York: Doubleday & Company, Inc., 1974.

This is typical far-out Goyen work. A charismatic preacher becomes an oil huckster. It's set near Houston.

Howard, Clark. *Dirt Rich*. New York: St. Martin's Press, 1988.

Dirt Rich is supposedly set in East Texas. It is not an East Texas that an East Texan would recognize. There aren't any black people in it, but there are lots of Choctaws from the reservation, who help the protagonist drill his well. Since there is no Indian reservation in East Texas, I had a difficult time taking this novel seriously. The protagonist, Sam Sheridan, also has the help of Pop Joyner in drilling the first well in East Texas. The enemy is Pete Spence, who owns a huge cattle ranch. None of this seemed believable.

Howard, Will. *Cyclone*: *South by Southwest*. Lubbock, Texas: Red Feather Publishing Company, 1979.

Cyclone is a disorganized novel. In the big scene at the end, a cylone hits the oilfield, killing Doris Ann Funts, the female part of a love triangle.

Lanham, Edwin. *Thunder in the Earth*. New York: Harcourt, Brace and Company, 1941.

This is an excellent novel. It begins in Oklahoma, so I am discussing it in my book on Oklahoma oil novels, *Sooner Boomers*.

Logan, Chauncey. *Burkburnett*. San Antonio: The Naylor Co., 1973.

Logan was a teenager in Burkburnett from 1917-24 during the oil boom there. This is not a particularly adept novel. Burkburnett is rather episodic, more like a biography of its central character, Jack Merrell, than a novel. Merrell arrives in Burkburnett on business, just in time to foil a bank robbery, rescuing Al LaFave, who immediately becomes his friend, and soon his business partner. They begin to buy leases in the area north of Burkburnett and bring in one of the first wells. Soon they have other wells and leases. Merrell is even the driller on one well although there is no evidence that he has worked on a rig before. Oil is discovered in Burkburnett itself, and soon the town is undergoing great changes. La-Fave and Merrell are the town leaders in trying to maintain some order in the midst of the boom. We have our usual oil-well fire and the description of fighting it. Unusual is the emphasis on the Influenza epidemic with the resultant problem of dealing with the orphans. The owner of the upscale Crystal Palace dance hall, Mary Dickens, raises money to build an orphanage. A local holiness church protests her having the orphanage, and in the turmoil Mary is shot. She recovers and eventually moves to Dallas, but not before she and Jack have fallen in love. Jack already has a family, and he has established them in a new home in Wichita Falls. Ultimately, the boom is over. Jack returns to his family, and they return to Burburnett.

Miller, Helen Topping. *Never Another Moon*. New York: Grosset and Dunlap, 1937.

Harriet Hale, daughter of famous Wildcatter Muncie Hale, gets out of an engagement with villainous fortune seeker and falls in love and marries a good honest driller. It's set somewhere in Texas, but the location is not distinguished well.

O'Neal, Cothburn. *Pa*. Crown Publishers, Inc.: New York, 1962.

Pa is an interesting study in point of view. It is told by a collective "we" which represents his grandchildren and youngest daughter. Pa Randall is the patriarch of the family and a real odd duck. He gives up farming his land in order to build a lake there. When oil is struck in East Texas, he befriends a wealthy oil man, helping him to get leases in the neighborhood. In turn, the oilman remodels Pa's lake cottage and rents it from him. Pa and the oilman travel about together, and everyone believes that Pa has become rich in the oil boom. The grandchildren grow up and prosper, and Pa lives a happy life. When he dies, the family is surprised to learn that Pa has little money, having never invested in oil himself. He has lived rather nicely on the rents from his lake cottage.

Obregon, Jay. *The Oilmen*. Cordovan Press: Houston, 1973.

In deep South Texas, Grady Kilgore and Charles Van Ulm try to drill a well although August Mann, a George Parr-like political kingpin, has vowed to stop them. When a group of Mann's men drive off their crew with most of their equipment, Kilgore captures some of Mann's men to help drill the well. Carlos Acero, Mann's second in command, at first refuses to work, but Kilgore will not feed him until he does. Finally, after the death of Van Ulm and a romance between Kilgore and Van Ulm's widow, the well is drilled though they have almost no supplies. Kilgore comes to accept the idea that Mexican-Americans can be good oilfield workers. And Acero, angry about Mann's unwillingness to free him, wrests power from Mann.

Pryor, Elinor. *The Big Play*. New York: McGraw-Hill, 1951.

This is a good oil novel. It has early scenes set in West Texas, but much of it is set in Oklahoma, so I discuss it in Sooner Boomers.

Smith, C. W. *Understanding Women*. TCU Press: Fort Worth, 1998.

It's 1956 and young Jimbo of Dallas gets a summer job with his Uncle Waylan. Uncle Waylan has several crews working in the oil patch in New Mexico. We are given a description of Jimbo first day on the job carrying pipe. Later one of the crew members is killed when a rig falls on him, but the novel is mostly about Uncle Waylan's deteriorating marriage and Jimbo's love for Trudy, his new girl friend.

Terrell, Esther McCord. *Oil Tide A Tale of Ranger*. Philadelphia: Dorrance & Company, 1945.

A nurse comes to the Ranger boomtown and immediately finds a great need for her training amid the casual violence of the street. She meets and marries a doctor.